SHARPSHOOTERS FOR HIRE

McGee and Salmon, two circus sharpshooters, flee New York where they face death because of unpaid gambling debts. Heading off west, the pair end up in the lawless town of Stoneville and become involved in a range war where one of the protagonists is a vicious madman. When they come face to face with a gang of train robbers they find their shooting skills are tested to the limit since they have to shoot men instead of just targets.

RON WATKINS

SHARPSHOOTERS FOR HIRE

Complete and Unabridged

LINFORD
Leicester

First published in Great Britain in 2002 by
Robert Hale Limited
London

First Linford Edition
published 2003
by arrangement with
Robert Hale Limited
London

British Library CIP Data

Watkins, Ron
    Sharpshooters for hire.—Large print ed.—
Linford western library
    1. Western stories
    2. Large type books
    I. Title
    823.9'14 [F]

    WES
    1500762

    ISBN 0–7089–9486–5

Published by
F. A. Thorpe (Publishing)
Anstey, Leicestershire

Set by Words & Graphics Ltd.
Anstey, Leicestershire
Printed and bound in Great Britain by
T. J. International Ltd., Padstow, Cornwall

This book is printed on acid-free paper

1

The two men stood facing each other. They were thirty yards apart, having first stood back to back, then each had taken fifteen paces before turning. Their hands were held poised above their revolvers.

'I'm calling you, you yellow-livered runt,' said the smaller of the two. His name was McGee and he was dressed in a white suit. He was wearing a white hat and below it the perspiration stood out on his brow.

'This is the last time you're going to call anyone,' said the other. His name was Salmon. He was taller than his opponent, but about the same age, both being in their late twenties. He was wearing a black Stetson.

'I'm going to count up to three,' said McGee.

'Are you sure you can count as far as

that?' sneered Salmon.

'One,' said McGee.

Salmon stared into his eyes. He knew that the eyes were always a give-away in a gun-fight. The split second before an opponent would draw he would tighten the muscles around the corners of his eyes. It was always a sure signal that he would be going for his gun.

'Two,' intoned McGee.

Salmon could feel the sweat on his brow now. He longed to wipe it away, but he knew that the next few seconds could mean the difference between life and death. He had been in such situations before and he would have thought that perhaps having experienced them they would somehow have become familiar and he would be able to take them in his stride. But no, here he was experiencing the usual dryness of the mouth, the almost overwhelming desire to lick his lips, the familiar tightness of the chest.

'Three,' McGee spat out.

They both went for their guns at the

very same moment. The sounds of their Colts were as one. There was a stunned silence for a moment as the results of their shooting-out became apparent.

McGee had shot Salmon's black hat off his head. Salmon had repeated the same treatment and his opponent's white hat had spiralled up into the air with a bullet-hole in it.

The watching audience burst into instantaneous applause. They clapped long and loud. They were a sophisticated New York audience and any show which brought a hint of the dangers of life in the Wild West was met with rapturous appreciation. And Horace Marney's Wild West Show did just that. Living in the warmth and elegance of their large town-houses they were avid for any knowledge about the rigours and dangers of life out West. The climax of the show in the display of shooting they had just witnessed gave them a thrill and emphasized the fact that the West was a dangerous place in which to live.

McGee and Salmon took their bows to increased applause. The two young ladies who had taken part in the show earlier with their horse-riding stunts came on to retrieve the hats. They joined hands with the two men and they all took another bow.

'Where are we going tonight?' whispered the blonde. Her name was Jill. She was tall and appeared to be quite pretty with her make-up and under the arc lamps, but on closer examination was not so attractive. She was Salmon's girlfriend.

'There's a new café opened in Forty-Second street,' said Letitia. She was McGee's girlfriend. She was short and dark with black, curly hair. She too was quite pretty with an almost gypsyish appearance.

'I think we'll give tonight a miss,' said McGee, as they left the arena.

'You're not short of money, are you?' demanded Letitia.

'Of course not,' replied McGee quickly. 'We were only paid the day before yesterday.'

Letitia glanced at him suspiciously. 'You're not thinking of going to a card-school are you, instead of taking us out?'

'Perish the thought,' said McGee.

'You'll be the one who'll perish if I find out that it's true,' snapped Letitia, who was known for her short temper.

'We just thought we'd have a quiet game of billiards tonight,' supplied Salmon. 'We'll ask around about the new café. If it's all right we'll take you there tomorrow.'

Jill accepted the idea more readily than Letitia. 'I want to wash my hair,' she stated.

'Well, all right,' Letitia agreed, grudgingly. 'But don't forget to come in and give me a good-night kiss when you come back. And heaven help you if I will be able to smell beer on you,' she added, warningly.

When they were out of earshot of their girlfriends, McGee said, 'We haven't got much time. Have you packed all your belongings?'

'Are you sure we're doing the right thing?' asked a worried Salmon.

'Of course we are,' said McGee positively. 'We agreed it was the only way out.'

'I don't like to leave the girls like this,' stated the other.

'We can't leave a note saying we've gone West,' said McGee, irritably. 'If we did they'd know where to find us.'

Salmon sighed. 'Yes, I suppose so.'

'Are you sure you've packed everything?' demanded McGee.

'It didn't take long,' said Salmon. 'It only took me about five minutes to put them in that old saddle-bag.'

They arrived at their tent. McGee realized that Salmon was having not only second thoughts but third ones as well about the wisdom of their leaving. He lit the lamp.

'Look at it this way,' he said. 'If Charlie the Hook finds out that we can't pay him the two-thousand dollars we owe him in gambling debts, we'll be dead meat. Our bodies will be found floating down the river. If we stay here that's what will happen to us.'

McGee's statement wiped the indecision from his friend's face.

'I never did like the water,' stated Salmon, as he picked up his old saddle-bag.

2

Later the same night McGee and Salmon were on a freight train heading west. They had jumped on the train at the first bend just outside the station, where the train had still been moving slowly. They were both comparatively agile since, during their spell with the circus, they had also taken part in the horse-riding act in which their girlfriends were the stars. They were in an empty carriage which was going west to pick up the cattle which was needed to feed the increasing population in New York.

'We might as well get some sleep,' said McGee, spreading out the blanket he had brought with him.

'I don't know how you can think of sleep at a time like this,' grumbled Salmon. 'We just left two lovely girls behind. Doesn't that mean anything to you?'

'Of course it does,' said McGee, as he stretched out on the blanket. 'It means we'll have to find two more girls when we get to Montana.'

'I don't see how you can take things so calmly,' said Salmon, angrily. 'I shouldn't have agreed to come on this train in the first place. In fact I think I'll jump off the train at the next bend.'

McGee sat up. 'Don't do anything stupid,' he stated, with alarm. 'Think of the consequences.'

'I am,' said Salmon, who was now standing by the open door.

McGee moved over to him. 'Think of the money we owe Charlie the Hook. Think of the two bodies floating down the river. *Our* bodies.'

'I'm sure we can come to some arrangement with Charlie,' stated Salmon, watching the line ahead. There was a full moon and he would be able to judge accurately the moment when he would jump from the train and roll down the bank.

'Yes, he'll arrange to kill you quickly

instead of using the hook which he has instead of his left hand.'

'I'll pay him back a hundred dollars at a time. It will be a few months before I finish paying him the thousand dollars I owe him, but at least I'll be back with the circus. And Jill.'

There was now a bend in sight. McGee saw it, too.

'There's one thing you should know before you jump,' said McGee.

'What's that?' demanded Salmon, giving his full attention to the approaching bend.

'The amount of money we owe Charlie the Hook,' stated McGee.

The bend was now approaching rapidly. 'So we owe him a few more hundred dollars,' stated Salmon, shifting the saddle-bag so that he would be ready to toss it out and then jump out after it.

'I wasn't going to tell you this,' said McGee. 'But it's a few thousand more we owe him. Not a few hundred.'

In spite of the fact that the train had

now began to slow as it approached the bend, Salmon turned.

'How much more do we owe him?' he shouted.

'Five thousand dollars.'

'What?' Salmon now gave McGee his full attention, ignoring the fact that the train was moving slowly round the bend.

'Here's the IOU.' McGee waved a piece of paper in front of Salmon's face. 'It says I owe Charlie the Hook five thousand dollars.'

'You swine,' yelled Salmon. 'You lying swine.'

'It doesn't make any difference,' said McGee, placatingly. 'Two thousand, five thousand.'

'I'll never speak to you again,' Salmon was still shouting.

McGee went back to his blanket. 'We'll start a new life out West. It'll work out, you'll see. You'll soon be thanking me for making you move out there.'

Salmon was still standing by the open

door. 'How did we come to owe him five thousand dollars?'

'It was on the last hand. You dropped out and went to the lavatory. You'd had a bad stomach all during the game. I had a king flush. I was sure I'd win.' McGee paused.

'What did he have?' demanded Salmon.

'Four aces,' stated McGee.

'Four aces,' said Salmon, bitterly. 'And because of that we're stuck on this train going nowhere.'

'We're going West,' stated McGee, positively. 'We're going to make a new start. We can ride and shoot. We're the sort of people they're looking for out West. It'll all work out, you'll see.'

'It better had,' said Salmon, bitterly. 'For your sake.'

3

Jill was weeping and Letitia was trying to comfort her. 'Where have they gone?' demanded Jill between sobs.

'It says here, 'We've gone West. Love from McGee and Salmon'.' Letitia re-read the grubby note.

'Love from Salmon.' Jill began to howl again.

'Why have they gone?' Letitia went outside the tent as if being out in the open would somehow provide the answer to her question. Jill followed her, still dabbing at her eyes. They had found the note pushed underneath the flap of their tent when they had got up.

'It must be something to do with their gambling,' continued Letitia, thoughtfully. There were several other tents in the circus and their occupants were beginning to stir. Some of them were going to the well to draw water in which to wash. They stared at Jill and Letitia curiously as they passed.

'The news will soon be all over the circus,' said a distraught Jill. 'What will folks say?'

'Never mind what folks will say. We've got to find out why they went.'

Jill knew that when Letitia was in this determined mood the only thing to do was to agree with her. 'How can we do that?' she asked, meekly.

'We go downtown to where they used to go to play billiards. Somebody there will know why they ran off like that.'

Half an hour later they were standing outside Henry's Billiard Room. A sign said MEN ONLY.

'We can't go in,' said Jill, with heartfelt relief. She hadn't been keen on venturing downtown in order to find out where their recalcitrant lovers had gone. It was obvious that they were probably never going to see them again. Having reached that conclusion she knew it would take her weeks to get over losing Salmon.

Letitia was knocking at the door. It was opened in a few moments by a weary figure who was as thin as the billiard cues inside the establishment.

'What do you want?' he demanded.

'I'm trying to find out about our friends, McGee and Salmon,' answered Letitia, with a winning smile.

'What about them?' The guardian of the billiard hall regarded them suspiciously.

'They've gone away,' said Jill, who felt that she should contribute something to the conversation.

'Gone away, have they?' sneered the other.

Letitia felt that he was a person to whom it would be easy to take a permanent dislike. Aloud she said, 'We think they owed somebody money.'

Yes, that was the obvious explanation, decided a sorrowful Jill. Salmon would never have left her like this unless he owed somebody money. But if that was so, why hadn't he come to her?

She could have let him have the few hundred dollars she had saved up. She had been putting it by until the day dawned when he would ask her to marry him. But now there was no chance of that. She began to weep.

'What's the matter with your friend?' The guardian jerked a thumb towards Jill.

'Never mind about her. What about McGee and Salmon?'

'They played cards with Charlie the Hook. Nobody in their right senses plays cards with Charlie the Hook.'

'They owed him money?' demanded Letitia.

'That's the word that got around.' The guardian seemed more friendly now.

'Did the word say how much they owed him?'

'Only that it was a few thousand.'

'A few thousand?' shrieked Jill.

'You'd better ask Charlie the Hook. He'll tell you exactly how much it was.'

'Where will we find him?' demanded

a determined Letitia.

'Listen, lady,' said the other, not unkindly. 'Where Charlie the Hook hangs out is not a suitable place for you two.'

'Let's go back,' said a worried Jill.

'Where does he hang out?' demanded Letitia.

'In a cellar.' He gave her details how to get there.

'Thanks.' Letitia started to move off, followed by a reluctant Jill.

They eventually found the cellar after taking a couple of false directions. It was an unprepossessing, low, one-storey building. Letitia hesitated outside the solitary brown door.

'Let's go back,' pleaded Jill.

'Not until we've seen Charlie the Hook,' replied Letitia, as she knocked at the door.

This time the guardian was a thick-set man who looked like a street-fighter. 'What do you want?' he snarled.

'We want to see Charlie the Hook,'

said Letitia, sounding more confident than she felt.

'Well you can't,' said the gorilla, preparing to shut the door.

'It's about McGee and Salmon,' said Letitia, quickly.

The door stayed partly open.

'Who is it?' shouted a voice from inside.

'Somebody who wants to see you about McGee and Salmon,' he shouted back.

There was a silence followed by the door opening from inside and a man materializing.

'What do you want?' demanded Charlie the Hook.

Letitia and Jill studied him. He was a balding, middle-aged man with a hard face. His unusual appendage of a hook instead of his left hand gave him a sinister appearance.

'Have you come with the money?' he demanded.

'How much is it?' demanded Letitia.

'You mean they haven't told you?'

sneered Charlie.

'Not the exact sum,' stated Jill. She thought he was a hateful man. How could Salmon have played cards with him?

'Not the exact sum.' Charlie tried to imitate her inflection without success.

'How much?' snapped Letitia.

'Five thousand dollars. I gave them to the end of the week. If they didn't come up with the money by then, I'd turn Hank and his brother loose on them. And Hank is a pussy-cat compared to his brother.'

They walked back to the circus in silence. When they arrived there Jill vented her anger.

'How could they play with such a horrible man?' she demanded, angrily.

'How could they lose so much money to him?' demanded Letitia.

'Five thousand dollars. They could never pay that back. The question is, what are we going to do next?'

'We're going to follow them,' said a determined Letitia.

'We're going to go West?' demanded a shocked Jill.

'We're not going to let them get away with it.'

'We can't go West. It's wild out there.'

'We haven't any choice. I've got to find McGee.'

'I'd like to see Salmon again too,' said a wistful Jill.

'You don't understand,' said Letitia. 'I've got to see McGee. I'm pregnant.'

'You're not?' said a surprised Jill.

'I am. The bastard.'

'Yes, men are bastards,' agreed Jill, with surprising venom.

'I want to make sure that our son or daughter is not a bastard as well,' stated Letitia, emphatically.

4

McGee and Salmon had lost track of time. They weren't sure how many days they had spent travelling west. They also didn't know how many trains they had jumped from one to another during their journey. They only knew that they had eventually reached the end of the line. The name of the town was Stoneville.

'It doesn't look much of a place,' grumbled Salmon, as they completed their usual manoeuvre of jumping off the train before it reached the station.

'The first thing I want is a hot bath,' said McGee.

'The first thing I want is a thick steak,' said Salmon.

They both satisfied their desires in the Long Horn saloon. They booked a room. They had dinner in the so-called dining-room which was really a section of the bar which had been partitioned off. However they had an excellent steak which even satisfied Salmon's appetite. Afterwards they bathed and found a barber's shop where they had their several days' growth of beard removed.

'I feel like a new man,' said Salmon, surveying himself in the barber's mirror.

'It's certainly an improvement,' agreed McGee. 'I was getting fed up of seeing you with that straggly beard.'

The barber interrupted their banter. 'You fellers wouldn't be looking for work, would you?'

'Well, yes, I suppose so,' said Salmon.

'You can ride?'

'Of course we can ride,' said McGee, scornfully.

'The Lazy Y ranch is looking for hands. It's owned by a rancher named Taunton. Tell him I sent you.' He didn't add that the rancher paid him ten dollars for each hand he sent to the ranch.

The next morning McGee and Salmon could be found walking the two miles or so to the ranch. The weather was fine. Although they had been constantly bickering on their long train journey, they strolled along contentedly together. As if by mutual consent they had put their disagreements behind them.

'Whatever he offers us, we'll take it,' said McGee. 'If we don't like the work we can always quit.'

The rancher turned out to be a middle-aged man with black hair and a beard and the sort of distinguished face that reminded Salmon of the pictures he had seen of the founding fathers.

'Have you two rode cattle before?' he demanded.

'Sure,' replied McGee.

Salmon's surprise at the lie was partly hidden by McGee's next quick question.

'How many do you have?'

'About five thousand,' said Taunton. 'You fellers are from back East?'

'New York,' supplied Salmon.

'Before we came out West a couple of years ago,' said McGee, quickly.

'You haven't been in trouble with the law, have you?' demanded Taunton, sharply.

'No,' they both replied, almost as one.

'I see you carry guns,' said Taunton, keenly. 'Do you know how to use them?'

'Sure, we know how to use them,' said McGee.

After they had been hired at the standard rate of ten dollars a week and all found, Taunton held a conversation with his manager, Cowley.

'There's something odd about those two guys I've just hired,' he stated. 'You'd better keep an eye on them. When I asked them if they could use guns, they both smiled, as if it was a joke. Maybe they're gunslingers.'

For the next few days, however, McGee and Salmon were more concerned with the stiffness of their limbs than practising their shooting. Although they were used to jumping on and off horses galloping round the circus ring, they found that sitting in the saddle and searching for stray cattle for hours at a time was a novel experience. For the first few days it left them with stiff limbs and they became the butts of the jokes of the other cowboys.

Although the comments about the greenhorns were regularly directed at them, there was nothing malicious about the other cowboys. McGee and Salmon found that they were a friendly bunch of guys. As the days went by and they became more proficient in the saddles the comments became fewer and fewer.

One day the other cowboys were gathered around the bunkhouse. McGee and Salmon had finished their roping early for a change and were sitting with them, enjoying a smoke. Suddenly one of the stallions which was known to be a bit wild jumped over the corral rails and celebrated its new-found freedom by appearing in front of the bunkhouse.

The cowboys were content to carry on smoking. It wasn't their problem to get the horse back into the corral. It was up to Cowley. He was the manager.

The stallion, instead of celebrating its freedom by galloping off towards the horizon, stayed where it was, contenting itself with snorting now and again and kicking up its heels. McGee stood up. The cowboys watched him as he went through the gate and walked towards the horse. Blackie, for that was the horse's name, also watched him balefully.

McGee had an apple in his hand. He held it out towards the stallion. Its reply was to snort several times and kick up its heels even more emphatically than before. McGee approached him steadily. When he was within a couple of feet he halted and held out the apple temptingly. The horse eyed the apple. McGee was speaking to it soothingly. The two stood stock still for ages. Suddenly the temptation of the apple became too much for Blackie. He put his muzzle in McGee's hand and grabbed it. At the same time he turned to gallop away with his prize. However McGee had other plans. He leapt up on to Blackie's back as the horse began to gallop off.

The cowboys, who until now had been casually watching the incident, now gave their full attention to McGee. He was riding Blackie bareback. It was a form of transport with which Blackie was not familiar, since his regular rider always put a saddle on him before riding off. Blackie's reaction was to try violently to unseat his rider. McGee hung on grimly. The cowboys cheered as the horse bucked and stood on its heels in an effort to unseat its unwelcome rider. McGee still clung on. The cowboys were shouting encouragement. Blackie's violent movements became fewer. He hadn't bargained for this when he had jumped over the corral fence. All he had wanted was a few minutes of freedom before he would allow himself to be led tamely back into the corral. His violent movements suddenly ceased. The cowboys threw their hats into the air and whooped with joy as McGee began to stroke Blackie's mane and speak to him soothingly.

Unseen to the cowboys Taunton and Cowley had come out of the house. They had watched McGee's efforts appreciatively.

'Are you thinking what I'm thinking?' asked Taunton.

'I think so,' said Cowley. 'There's a rodeo coming up in a couple of weeks' time. We haven't had anybody we can enter for it. But I think we've found one now.'

'You could be right,' said Taunton, thoughtfully.

5

Cowley broke the news to McGee and Salmon that there was going to be a rodeo in a couple of weeks' time.

'I've never been to a rodeo,' said Salmon.

'I thought you fellers said you've been out West for a couple of years,' stated Cowley. 'It's strange you haven't seen a rodeo.'

'We don't go much for cruelty to animals,' said McGee, quickly. 'Anyhow we spend most of our spare time playing cards.'

'It's not the animals who suffer,' said Cowley. 'It's the riders. Unless of course they're good enough,' he added, with a keen glance at McGee.

'Yes, I suppose they have to be pretty good,' agreed McGee. Privately he wondered where the conversation was leading.

'The boss and I saw you riding Blackie yesterday,' said Cowley.

Salmon jerked a thumb in McGee's direction. 'He was showing off as usual,' he stated.

'The question is would you like to show off in the rodeo ring?' Cowley directed the question at McGee.

McGee laughed. 'I can ride a bit, but I'm not that good.'

'Of course you are,' said Salmon, needling him. 'You always said you were the best rider the circus ever had.'

'You two worked in a circus?' demanded Cowley, keenly.

'That was before we came out West a couple of years ago,' said McGee, shooting a baleful glance at Salmon.

'Well, what do you think?' demanded Cowley.

'I'd have to stay on the back of a horse for as long as I could?' queried McGee.

'A horse which hasn't been broken,' Cowley pointed out.

'Go on. You can do it,' said Salmon.

'The worst that can happen is that you'd break an arm or a leg.'

McGee scowled at him. 'What's in it for me?' he demanded.

'There's a two hundred dollars prize money,' said Cowley, casually.

'Two hundred dollars? He'll do it,' said Salmon.

'Hold on,' said McGee. '*I'm* the one who makes the decision.'

'The boss will give you time off from riding the range during the next two weeks so that you can concentrate on the rodeo,' continued Cowley, remorselessly.

'I suppose there'll be some betting on the results,' said McGee, thoughtfully.

'There always is,' supplied Cowley.

'Of course, since I'm an unknown quantity, I expect the odds against me winning would be pretty high?'

'I would say they would be long odds,' agreed Cowley. 'Well, what shall I tell the boss?'

'Tell him he'll do it,' announced Salmon.

Cowley stared at McGee for confirmation.

'What have I to lose? Apart from a few broken bones?' he stated.

A quarter of an hour later Cowley was seated in Taunton's study. They were smoking cigars.

'What do you think of his chances?' demanded Cowley.

'He let slip that he used to work in a circus. In fact they both did,' said Cowley. 'That's why he's a good horseman.'

'So they used to work in a circus,' said Taunton, thoughtfully. 'I thought there was something odd about them.'

'We've got about half a dozen horses which haven't been broken,' stated the other. 'He can practise on those during the next two weeks.'

'It would be great if we can put one over on the Tall T ranch,' said his boss. 'I've been wanting to get even with them for ages.'

'You mean you've been wanting to take over their ranch,' stated Cowley.

'How do you know that?' snapped Taunton. For a moment his *bonhomie* slipped. It was as if a mask had been torn from his face.

'I keep my ear to the ground,' said Cowley. Privately he wondered whether he had gone too far. Sometimes when his boss's mask slipped he appeared to be an entirely different person. In some cases a frightening one.

However, Taunton's expression returned to his normal pleasant one with his next remark.

'Yes, maybe McGee will come in useful for us,' he stated.

6

'It will mean there'll be a lot of innocent people killed,' said Quail. He was a tall figure who always wore black. More than a few times in his thirty-odd years on earth he had been mistaken for a preacher. In fact his parents had always wanted him to preach from the pulpit. Instead he had chosen to become a leader of men in a different calling — that of a robber.

'That'll be their bad luck,' said Lille.

'Maybe there won't be too many killed — perhaps just a few,' suggested Frenchie. The rest of the gang sat in a circle round their camp-fire and listened as their leaders discussed the question.

'If anybody's got any doubts about going ahead with the robbery, then they'd better say so now,' said Quail.

There were fourteen men in the

gang. Nearly all of them were wanted in various states for robbery or murder, most of them in fact for both robbery and murder. They glanced at each other suspiciously. Most of them had never been too concerned about how many people they had killed in the past. They couldn't see that it would make any difference now.

'Right, then that's settled,' said Quail.

The general feeling of relief was interrupted by a voice from the back of the company.

'Isn't there some way that we can make sure that not too many people are killed?'

Quail quickly identified the speaker. 'I see you've got some reservations, Hislop,' he sneered.

'Well, maybe if we put less explosives on the line it would mean that the train would only jump the rails. That way only a few people would get killed.'

'You're forgetting the guards on the train,' said Lille. He was a ruthless killer who had operated single-handed for most of his forty years. Then a few years before he had been involved in a gunfight over a disputed hand of cards. His opponent had drawn his gun quicker, but Lille had already had him covered with the gun in his left hand under the table. Although the other had outdrawn him Lille had killed him with the gun in his left hand. It had taught him a lesson, though. He was no longer quick enough to succeed in single-handed gunfights. So at the first opportunity he had joined up with a gang. In his case Quail's gang.

'There'll be enough confusion with a smaller explosion to distract the guards on the train,' continued Hislop, stubbornly. 'When we move in we'll be able to take the guards. Then we help ourselves to the gold and money as planned.'

Quail stood up. All the others were still seated on the ground. He walked over to Hislop. He stood over him and posed the question.

'How long have you been with us?'

'About six months,' replied the other. He stared up at the gaunt face above him. He felt at a disadvantage sitting down while Quail peered down at him.

'In that six months how many successful robberies have we committed?' continued Quail, remorselessly.

'Two,' admitted Hislop.

'Two,' Quail spat the words out. 'Only two. We've just made enough from those bank robberies to keep us together for the past few months. That's right, isn't it?' He leaned over Hislop and put his face close to his.

Hislop instinctively turned away. Quail had been chewing wild garlic and the smell was nauseating. 'Yes,' he admitted, regretfully.

'Here we have a chance to make a killing — a real killing. I'm not talking about the guards on the train.' The gang chuckled at his wit. 'This is the chance I've been waiting for for years. A train loaded with gold and money coming west from New York. Most of the small local banks have been bought up by one

37

firm — Western Bank Alliance. Now they are going to stock up these banks with enough gold and money to help them to expand. Only it will never reach its destination. Because we will be blowing up the train. Now I don't care if we kill a few dozen people. We've got to make sure that this is going to be a big explosion, not a small firework-display. So either you're with us, Hislop, or you can saddle your horse and leave now.'

He straightened up and stared at the figure sitting on the ground. Their eyes met. There was contempt in Quail's gaze. He couldn't stand a man with a conscience.

'I'm with you,' said Hislop, through tight lips. He had read the contempt in Quail's gaze and had quickly realized the precariousness of his position. If he had followed his instinct and decided to leave the gang, it was probable that Quail would have shot him in the back before he had reached his horse. Quail would never let anyone leave the gang in case he squealed to the authorities. Hislop knew that from now on if he wished to remain a live member of the gang he would have to tread a thin line.

7

'You've done what?' yelled McGee.

'All right, there's no need to shout,' remonstrated Salmon.

The conversation was taking place outside the saloon named The Three Horseshoes. The two had been on their way there when Salmon dropped his bombshell.

'You've sent them a telegram?' McGee was still shouting.

'Just to say that we're both well.' Salmon was less sure of himself now.

'And I suppose you said where we are?' McGee's voice dripped with sarcasm.

'Of course not,' countered Salmon. 'How stupid do you think I am?'

'Do I have to answer that? The address of the telegraph office would be on the telegraph form. They'd know it came from Stoneville.'

'I never thought of that.' Salmon had

the grace to look shamefaced.

'You never thought of that,' echoed McGee, scornfully.

'Well, anyhow, there's no harm done. They'd never think of following us here.'

'Letitia would. She's as stubborn as a mule.'

'They're hundreds of miles away. They'd have to come by train. It would cost a fortune. They'll never come,' said Salmon, reassuringly.

'You'd better be right,' scowled McGee.

'Come on. Let's play cards,' suggested Salmon. 'Let's take some more money off the cowboys.'

McGee allowed himself to be led inside the saloon.

★ ★ ★

The reactions of Jill and Letitia were mixed when they received the telegram. 'It's nice to know that they are both well,' stated Jill.

41

'Where's Stoneville?' demanded Letitia.

Jill examined the telegram. 'It says here that the telegram is from Stoneville, Montana.'

'Montana,' said Letitia, thoughtfully.

'It's a long way off,' said Jill. 'We couldn't consider going there.'

'How did McGee and Salmon get there?' demanded Letitia. She answered their own question. 'By train.'

'We're not going to jump train?' Jill looked at her askance.

'Of course not,' said Letitia, trying unsuccessfully to conceal her irritation. 'How much money have we got?'

'I've got a few hundred,' said Jill, warily.

'I've got a few hundred as well,' stated Letitia more positively. 'We'd have enough to get us to Stoneville.'

'I don't know,' said an undecided Jill. 'I don't like the idea of going from New York.'

'You love Salmon, don't you?' Letitia had suddenly become persuasive.

'Of course I do. I'm mad about the big feller.'

'I feel the same way about McGee. The skunk,' retorted Letitia.

'Well, maybe we could go after them.' Jill was wavering.

'There's another thing,' stated Letitia. ' I'm pregnant. I want to marry McGee before our child is born.' For the first time she showed a hint of feminine weakness. Jill put her arm around her to comfort her.

'Are you all right?' she demanded.

'Yes, I'm all right,' stated Letitia, blowing her nose vigorously. She never liked showing weakness. Among her ancestors, the gypsies, it had always been regarded as behaviour belonging to children.

'Are you sure you'll be all right to travel to Montana in your condition?' Her friend still expressed concern.

'I'm only three months' pregnant,' stated Letitia. 'I'm not going to have the baby on the way.'

'No, I don't suppose you would be,' retorted her friend.

'There's one other thing. Horace said

he's only keeping us on until the end of the month. We'll be out of a job then. If we stay here, what are we going to do?'

It was a powerful argument which Jill didn't try to counter. 'When do we go to the station to book our tickets?' she demanded.

This time it was Letitia's turn to give her friend a hug. 'There's no time like the present,' she replied.

They booked their tickets on the train which was going the following day.

'The fare wasn't as much as I thought it would be,' announced Jill.

'I expect the fare is cheap because nobody wants to go to Stoneville,' retorted Letitia.

They next day they arrived early to catch the train. However the train was already waiting in the station. There were a couple of dozen soldiers who were standing around. It seemed as though they were waiting for someone.

'Here are some empty seats.' Letitia led the way into the compartment. There was only a middle-aged man in a grey striped suit sitting in one of the corner seats.

They put their cases up on the rack. Jill sat on one of the seats while Letitia went to the window to look out.

'We should be off soon,' suggested Jill, hopefully.

'They're carrying some chests into the last carriage,' Letitia announced. 'They seem to be heavy.'

'They should be,' said the man. 'They're carrying a consignment of gold and money for the banks out West.'

8

McGee was riding the range. He liked the sense of freedom that came with it. He was a few hundred yards away from the next cowboy. All he had to do was to keep an eye out for any stray steers. If he found one with the Lazy Y brand on it, he had to rope it and take it back to the herd which was about half a mile away. There was usually no difficulty in roping the steer. They were docile animals and would allow themselves to be led meekly back to the herd.

Although they had only been on the ranch for a couple of weeks, he had settled easily into the new way of life. Of course he missed the excitement of the circus. He missed the applause which greeted the shooting act between himself and Salmon. And of course he missed Letitia. They got on well together, although she had rather a sharp tongue. But he could overlook that fault in her character since she more than made up for it when they made love. Not that they had many opportunities in the close-knit group of the circus. But when they did manage to sneak away from the others she allowed him to enjoy her body with complete abandonment.

He was thinking about one of those delicious moments when there was the unmistakable sound of a rifle-shot. The bullet that whistled past his ear told him that he was the target. The horse automatically reared. McGee steadied it and instinctively slid from the saddle, clinging to the side of the horse and keeping it between himself and the direction from which the bullet had come. He didn't stay to find out whether there was going to be another bullet. He rode hell for leather back towards the ranch.

One of the cowboys spotted him. He shouted out, 'What's up, McGee?'

'Some bastard shot at me,' came the

reply, as he slid from the horse down to the ground.

'I thought I heard a shot,' said the cowboy. His name was Jones and from his accent he had some Welsh ancestory among his forefathers.

'The shot came from the direction of the Tall T ranch. Why should someone take a shot at me?'

'I shouldn't think they're trying to kill you. Whoever shot at you could probably have killed you if he was really trying.'

'Thanks. You certainly know how to cheer somebody up,' snapped McGee.

'It's probably all to do with the rodeo,' explained Jones.

'They told me it could be dangerous riding the horses. They didn't tell me that I was going to be shot at as well.'

'I don't think he intended to kill you. All he was trying to do was to make you fall from your horse. Anyhow, that was great riding, hanging on to the side of the horse like that.'

'So the idea was that I would fall off

my horse, maybe break a bone or two. That way I would be out of the rodeo,' said McGee, slowly and thoughtfully.

'That's what it looks like to me,' replied Jones. 'As I said, if he was trying — '

'Yeah, I know,' said McGee quickly.

Back in the ranch they were met by Cowley. 'I thought I heard some shooting.' He addressed the remark to McGee.

'Somebody took a pot shot at me. Jones says it was one of the Tall T outfit,' replied McGee, as he disappeared inside the bunkhouse. A few minutes later he reappeared, strapping on his gun belt.

'You're not going out looking for trouble are you?' demanded a worried Cowley.

'No, but I intend looking after myself if trouble comes my way,' said McGee, drawing his Colt with lightning speed and taking imaginary aim at a distant object.

Jones whistled appreciatively. 'Say,

can you shoot that thing as well as you can draw?' he demanded.

McGee looked around for a suitable target. His gaze finally settled on a row of pegs strung out on a line in front of the bunkhouse. There were a couple of dozen or so of them spaced out along the line. They would be the recipients of the cowboys' shirts and underwear after they had had their weekly bath. McGee walked up to them. Cowley and Jones watched him expectantly. He turned his back on the line and began to walk away. He took fifteen paces then stopped. The two men held their breath. Suddenly McGee spun round and in a flurry of gunfire hit six of the pegs, smashing them completely.

He calmly replaced the Colt in its holster.

'Boy, was that some shooting,' enthused Jones.

Cowley was no less impressed. 'That's the best shooting I've seen for ages,' he announced.

'Can you get a message to the Tall T

ranch?' McGee asked Jones.

'Sure, I can ride over there any time. As long as I've got permission.'

Cowley nodded to show that it was granted.

'Tell them that whoever took a pot shot at me had better not try it again. If they do I'll shoot his ears off.'

'I'll be happy to take the message,' said Jones, with a wide grin. 'Those Tall T riders are getting too big for their boots.'

McGee turned to go back into the bunkhouse. Cowley called to him.

'When you've put your guns away come inside the house to see the boss. I think we might be able to find you a more rewarding job than just roping stray steers.'

9

Staunton Carter, deputy of the Pinker-ton Detective Agency was hopping mad. His unfortunate assistant, Larry Pike, had to bear the brunt of his anger.

'You know what this means,' shouted Carter. He banged his desk to empha-size the point.

'I can make a good guess,' said Pike. He was a very tall, thin man who walked with a perpetual stoop as though apologizing for his excessive height.

'It means war,' yelled his boss. He was a rugged, middle-aged man who had put the fear of God into many of his subordinates. He was now doing the same with Pike.

'I think that's a bit strong, isn't it?' replied Pike, defensively. He was standing in front of his boss's desk. Usually he would have been told curtly to sit down, but having delivered his unpalatable news he had been left standing. He now shuffled from one foot to the other uncomfortably.

'It means we'll never trust the Press again. It means we'll never consult another editor. It means we'll never let a reporter into this building. To me that's war. I suppose you'd call it a little skirmish.'

'Maybe nothing will come of it,' suggested the other, with more hope than expectancy.

Carter picked up the telegram from his desk. He handled it carefully between his two fingers as though it were contaminated. He read it aloud. He had let Pike read it when the unfortunate subordinate had originally brought it into his office.

'It's from Epping, in our New York office. It says 'The delivery of gold and money from the New York bank to the Western banks has been leaked to the Press. The *New York Argus* printed an article about it. Expect repercussions'.'

He dropped the telegram on to his desk.

With the descent of the telegram to the polished mahogany desk came silence. Pike inwardly prayed that it would continue for some time. His prayer wasn't answered, since Carter yelled, 'Expect repercussions.'

Pike nodded. He knew that anything he said would only inflame his superior's temper. The only other option was to contribute as few words as possible to the situation, on the assumption that the fewer words he contributed, the less fuel there would be to fan the flames of his boss's terrible mood.

'Expect repercussions.' Carter thumped the desk again. 'We'll have repercussions from the Quail gang, the Scarne gang, the Springer gang, every gang of outlaws in the West with one of their members who can read a newspaper.'

Pike kept silent.

'I'll bet my retirement pension that the gold will never arrive at its destination. In fact it probably won't get within a few hundred miles of it,' he concluded, bitterly.

Pike again contributed nothing.

'What's the matter with you? Cat got your tongue?' snarled Carter.

'I was just thinking . . . ' ventured Pike.

'What profound thoughts have you to contribute to this — unbelievable cock-up?'

Pike knew that this was usually the second phase of his superior's tirade. When he descended to sarcasm it meant that the initial outburst was almost over.

'Well, there are a couple of dozen soldiers on the train. They should be able to handle the situation.'

'Should be able to handle the situation,' Carter repeated, with massive sarcasm. 'Are you just stupid or pretending to be stupid?' Pike waited for the next pronouncement. It was obvious that Carter was not going to let the matter rest. 'Have you thought how any one of these gangs is going to stop the train? No, I don't suppose you have. Your mental processes don't run beyond looking after your daily needs.'

Pike raised his own voice for the first time. 'That's not fair,' he protested.

Carter ignored him. 'They're going to blow up the train. They'll guess that the gold and money is in the last carriage — it's a wonder that the reporter in the newspaper didn't notify them of that fact — so they'll stop the train by putting explosives on the line. The engine will come off the rails. Some of the carriages will concertina into others. There will be mayhem. Dozens of people will be killed. The gang will pick off the soldiers as they jump from the train. Then afterwards they will calmly collect the gold and money and ride away.'

Pike paled at the picture his superior had painted. It was going to be a tragedy on a massive scale. Lots of innocent people were going to be killed. And there was nothing that anyone could do about it.

10

McGee and Salmon were seated in the drawing-room of the ranch house, smoking cigars. They were the guests of honour of their boss, Taunton. They were seated in comfortable armchairs. The only thing that was missing in McGee's estimation was a glass of whiskey. But he had discovered a couple of days ago that Taunton was a teetotaller, and so he had not expected any strong drink. The cigar, though, was thick and obviously expensive. He puffed it appreciatively.

'I've heard from Cowley that you boys are handy with guns,' said Taunton, coming straight to the point.

'We used to be in a circus,' McGee explained. 'We used to shoot at each other.'

'As part of the act,' Salmon elaborated.

'I don't know whether you know it,

but the Tall T ranch have been stealing our cattle for some time,' said Taunton, looking at them thoughtfully.

'The boys in the bunkhouse have mentioned it,' said McGee.

'I don't mind the odd steer now and again. After all I've got five thousand head of cattle. But lately the steers have been disappearing at an alarming rate.'

'What do they do after they've taken the steers?' asked Salmon.

'They change the brand mark. It's easy to change a Lazy Y into a Tall T brand. You'd never know the difference.'

'What would you want us to do?' demanded McGee.

'Ride the range wearing your guns. As you know I don't allow any of my cowboys to carry guns. Anyhow they wouldn't know how to use them. But you two fellers could carry guns — with my permission.'

'You wouldn't expect us to shoot at anyone, would you?' asked a concerned Salmon.

Taunton smiled. 'No, that's the sort of stuff that you read about in the dime magazines. What will happen is you will carry your guns. I will get the word to Stiles that you are gunslingers — which in a sense you are. I think it could well dissuade him from stealing my steers in future.'

'Do we get paid extra for this?' enquired McGee. Salmon glanced at him appreciatively. He hadn't thought of that. Trust McGee to turn the situation to their advantage.

'Double what I'm paying you at the moment,' said Taunton, without turning a hair. 'If that's agreeable.'

They both nodded.

'Right, then you'll start tomorrow. You'll be riding the part of the range near to the Tall T spread.'

Back in the bunkhouse the two sat on a bench and discussed the sudden change in their fortunes.

'Twice the pay, just for carrying our guns,' said Salmon.

'It sounds all right,' said McGee.

'If you hadn't given the demonstration of your shooting by hitting all those pegs, we wouldn't have been given the job,' admitted Salmon.

'I wonder if there's any snag about it.' McGee's face wore a thoughtful expression.

'What snags can there be?' demanded Salmon. 'We'll be getting money for old rope.'

'When we're out on the range, we'll make sure we'll stick together,' stated McGee.

'We always have,' stated Salmon, positively.

If they could have overheard the conversation which was at that moment taking place in the drawing-room they had not long quitted they would have been very concerned.

Cowley had taken the place of the two and was now smoking a cigar with Taunton.

'So what do you think?' he demanded.

'I think you've come up with a solution to our problem,' admitted his boss.

'McGee can certainly shoot,' confirmed Cowley. 'He says that Salmon is just as good as he is.'

'It's the chance we've been waiting for.' For the first time there was excitement in Taunton's voice.

'Yes, it would be nice to get rid of Stiles once and for all. If we could take over his ranch we would have better access to water. The river runs for most of its course through his land.'

'I've offered to buy his ranch on three occasions,' stated Taunton. 'I've put up the price each time, but he refuses to accept my offers.'

'We've pushed him into a corner several times, but he's refused to budge,' confirmed his manager.

'That's probably why one of his men shot at McGee,' continued Taunton. 'Anyhow, we can go ahead with our next plan. It will stir up a range war between us and Stiles. We've got over twice as many men as him. And the sheriff is on our side. We should be able to drive Stiles off the range for good.

He'll wish he had accepted my last offer for his ranch.' For the first time his face wore a nasty scowl. McGee and Salmon wouldn't have recognized the expression from the usual pleasant face they had witnessed in the drawing-room.

'Don't forget you've promised me the Stiles's ranch if we pull this off,' said Cowley.

'I won't forget,' promised Taunton.

11

Letitia and Jill had spent a couple of hours on the train. What had started off as an exciting adventure, since neither of them had been on a long journey before, had now become a boring routine. The seats were hard and not particularly comfortable. The only slight advantage they experienced at present was that, apart from their original companion, nobody else had entered their compartment when the train had stopped at stations.

From time to time Jill glanced at her friend to confirm that she was feeling all right. Letitia found these enquiring glances a source of irritation, but managed to conceal her annoyance. In fact she was feeling fine and wondered whether she was over the first few uncomfortable weeks.

Their travelling companion had been

silent after imparting the initial information that the train was carrying both gold and money. He had contented himself with smoking small thin cigars. Now he coughed with the obvious intention of making conversation.

'How far are you ladies going?' he demanded.

'All the way to Montana,' stated Letitia.

'You've got a long journey then,' said the man. 'By the way, my name is Daley. Bruce Daley.' The two companions introduced themselves. 'I'm going to Chicago,' said Daley. 'I work in theatres. I'm going to Chicago to take over an old theatre and to improve it. We're going to put gas-lamps inside instead of oil-lamps.'

For the next half-hour or so he talked enthusiastically about the theatres he had helped to renovate. Some of them were in New York and Jill and Letitia were familiar with them. When he had finally come to the end of describing his successes he asked the ladies if they had an occupation.

'We're entertainers,' said Letitia. 'But not in theatres.'

She described to him their act in the circus.

'I'm impressed,' he said. 'If you ever end up in Chicago, here's my card.' He handed it to them. 'I'll be there for the next few months.'

'We're going to Montana to join up with our boyfriends,' explained Jill.

'Oh, I see, they've settled down in Montana and they've sent for you to join them.'

'Not exactly. They don't know we're coming,' said Letitia.

Daley looked puzzled.

'They left us in the lurch,' explained Jill. 'They set off west without us knowing.'

'We're going to give them a big surprise when we catch up with them,' stated Letitia, emphatically.

'Well I must say you are two very brave young ladies,' Daley replied. 'I'm very impressed.'

They eventually reached Chicago.

'This is where you get off,' said Letitia.

'Listen,' said Daley. 'The train will be here for about half an hour while it's drawing water. Why don't you two ladies go and find some food in one of the market stalls by the station. I'll look after your luggage while you're away.'

Jill looked at Letitia doubtfully.

'I could certainly do with something to eat,' her friend announced.

'I promise you I will look after your luggage,' said Daley. 'I'm not in any hurry. I can wait until you return.'

'All right,' said Letitia. 'We'll be back as soon as possible.'

They made their way to the food stalls outside the station. One particular stall was serving some deliciously smelling rabbit stew.

'Let's have some,' said Letitia, excitedly.

There were several people waiting to be served and Jill kept casting anxious eyes at the train. It was finally their turn to be served. The stall-owner, an Irishman named O'Leary, handed them the dish with the deliciously smelling stew inside.

'Don't forget I want the dish back,' he informed them.

The train whistled while they were only halfway through eating the meal.

'It's all right,' said O'Leary. 'That's the first whistle. It won't be going for about another ten minutes.'

Jill was all for handing the unfinished meal back to the stall-owner and hurrying to catch the train. But Letitia restrained her.

'We've got time to finish our meal. And anyhow we probably won't be getting anything to eat for hours.'

Jill dutifully gulped down the rest of the stew. The train gave another whistle.

'My God, it's going,' she shrieked.

The train gave its usual preparatory jerk before moving off.

'Wait for us,' screamed Letitia, as they hared towards it.

12

McGee wasn't any less vociferous when Salmon confessed that he had received a telegram from Jill.

'What, she sent you a telegram?' he yelled.

'I only had it this morning,' explained his companion.

'I suppose it stated they were both well,' stated a sarcastic McGee.

'She said she was all right.'

'What about Letitia?' Concern had crept into his voice.

'She said she was all right — considering.'

'Considering what? Are you holding anything back from me?'

Salmon dropped the bombshell. 'Letitia is expecting a baby.'

'What!' McGee was yelling again.

'Letitia is expec — '

'I heard what you said,' stated a calmer McGee.

68

'You didn't know this before we set off?'

'Of course I didn't. Think of it, Letitia is expecting my baby. I wonder if it will be a boy.'

'Well, you'll have a chance to find out soon. They're both on their way here. That was the other thing Jill said.'

To his surprise McGee accepted the news with equanimity. He was still in a half-trance after having received the news about the baby.

'Perhaps it will work out after all,' he said, dreamily.

'I thought you said that the idea was that we came here to get away from our girlfriends,' remonstrated Salmon.

'Yes, but this changes everything. We came here in the first place to get away from Charlie the Hook.'

'You soon change your tune,' said Salmon, scornfully.

'Think of it,' said McGee, reasonably. 'When we came from New York we were broke. Now we've come to Stoneville we're earning good money.

69

Taunton is paying us double what we were having just for carrying our guns. Then there's the rodeo coming up. When I win that I'll have a nice fat bonus. It will all come in handy to buy things for the baby.'

'*If* you you win the rodeo,' supplied Salmon.

'Of course I'll win,' stated McGee, positively. 'It shows that the others are worried about me winning otherwise they wouldn't have taken a pot shot at me. Anyhow I don't see what you're complaining about. You'll be glad to see Jill, won't you? After all you're the one who's been sending the telegrams.'

'Of course I'll be glad to see Jill. I love her.'

'Well, there you are then. Everything has worked out for the best after all.'

They both fell silent after McGee's pronouncement. They were riding the range, keeping near to the land to the north which belonged to Stiles. They could not see the Stiles ranch, which was about half a mile away, hidden by a stand of poplar trees.

'Taunton said it would be better if we split up,' said Salmon.

'Yeah, I suppose so,' concurred McGee. 'You go on ahead. I'll go back the way we've come.' He turned the horse around and let it retrace its steps at a slow trot. Truth to tell he was so busy with his thoughts that he didn't notice the horse's movements. Letitia was expecting a baby. *His* baby. It meant that he would be a father. Of course that would change his life. He knew that he would have to accept new responsibilities. Not only that but he would have to give up things, such as gambling. Well, he was sure his son would be worth the sacrifice. It was funny how he was already thinking of the baby as a son. *His son*. The words seem to roll pleasantly off his tongue. It was a good thing there was nobody within a few hundred yards of him to hear him saying the words to himself. He tried them out again. Yes, they even sounded better by repetition.

There was the sound of a shot. Salmon, who was not too far away to be out of sight, turned in the saddle. He was just in time to see McGee topple from his horse.

13

The members of the Quail gang were waiting impatiently for the train to appear. They were concealed on either side of the railway line. Their positions had been chosen carefully so that they were spaced out and hidden from any watchers on the train by thicket bushes. When the right time came they would be able to pick off the soldiers as they left the last carriage.

Their position had also been chosen carefully in relation to the bend in the line which was visible in the distance. It was important that the dynamite on the track should explode just before the engine reached it. The result would be that the track would buckle, the engine driver would not be able to brake in time and the train would be thrown off the track. Since there was an embankment to the left of the track the weight of the engine would pull several of the carriages with it. This would add to the pandemonium caused by the explosion.

The person in charge of the dynamite was a man named Ablet. He was a thin weasel-faced man who had worked in many coal mines in Pennsylvania. He knew all about fuses and how much he should allow in order that the train, which would travel four hundred yards from the time it appeared round the corner to his hiding place, would be blown up. He knew it was four hundred yards because he had paced it not once, but twice, to make sure that his calculations were correct.

Hislop, the member of the gang who had most reservations about the loss of life which was pending, surveyed the deserted track like the rest. The rewards were going to be incredible — far beyond his wildest dreams. He would have enough money to ensure that he didn't have to become involved in another robbery for the rest of his life. He'd probably even have money to spare. Perhaps he could put the money to some good use. In order to atone for the people on the train who were going to be killed. Perhaps he would help to build a church with it. There was always a demand for money to build churches in the West. The towns were expanding so quickly that they were always advertising in local papers for contributions in order to help local people build their church. Yes, that was an idea! He seized on it avidly. He would give some of the money he was going to get from the robbery to help build a church somewhere or other.

Quail, in between watching for the train in the distance, kept glancing at Hislop. He had deliberately positioned himself next to him so that he could keep an eye on him. He had his suspicions about Hislop. How would he respond when the time came? Would he play his part in picking off the soldiers? If there was any doubt about Hislop's response to the train crash then Quail had decided to act himself. He would shoot his companion. He would have no compunctions about it. He wanted members of his gang to be one hundred per cent with him. Any waverer would be dealt with instantly. And with fatal consequences for them.

Frenchie stared unblinkingly at the line ahead. He was eagerly anticipating the fight. He was a soldier — or rather he had been a soldier until he had been forced out of the army. At his court martial his commanding officer had denied that he had been 'picked on' because he was the only Frenchman in his division. He had admitted that he had assaulted his superior officer, but the man had been such a swine that he had it coming to him. After all he had only knocked him out. He had actively considered slitting his throat. It was the sort of retaliation which he had deserved after the way he had treated him. The worse thing was, though, that none of his so-called friends had stood by him. Fair-weather friends, all of them. Well, now he would have his chance to get his own back on them. Of course they wouldn't be the same soldiers on the train, but they were all tarred with the same brush. If he had been in their division he was sure that they wouldn't have stood by him either. Then he had had that piece of luck when he had been able to escape from the soldiers during a storm when they were transferring him to the prison camp. Yes, he really was looking forward to picking them off as they jumped off the wrecked train.

It seemed an eternity before the train whistled, indicating that it was going to come round the bend. His hands had become sticky while waiting for it. He wiped them on his trousers. As the train appeared he gripped his Winchester comfortably but tightly as he had trained to do in the army.

14

'If we only knew where the gang was going to strike,' said Carter. 'But it could be anywhere along a thousand miles of railway.'

'So you're sure there's going to be an attack on the train?' asked Pike.

'Of course there will be,' said Carter, emphatically. 'There's no doubt about it.'

Pike was seated in his boss's office. The fact that he had been offered a seat meant that Carter's anger at the announcement in the Press had finally evaporated. Carter was now willing to discuss the matter rationally.

'If, as you say, they get away with the money and gold we'll have to mount the biggest manhunt we have so far undertaken,' said his assistant.

'We haven't got the resources to mount a full-scale manhunt,' said

Carter, in a voice tinged with regret. 'Not unless Mr Pinkerton can come up with some more staff.'

'That means we'll have to depend on bounty hunters,' stated Pike.

'That's how it appears. We've had to depend on them before and it looks as though we'll have to do it again.'

'The railway companies are making enough to give us more money to employ more staff,' suggested Pike.

'A lot will depend on Epping,' said Carter, thoughtfully.

'In what way?' asked Pike.

'He'll be on the train. When the news that the train would be carrying the money was released to the whole world, I telegraphed to him to tell him to catch the train.'

This was news to Pike. However he did not display any reaction. He had long ago learned that any show of emotion would be seized up by his boss if he was in a bad mood and used to his detriment.

'Let's hope he doesn't get killed in

the robbery — if there is one.'

'His main purpose is to stay alive, and hopefully give us some information about the gang who attacked the train,' stated Carter.

At that moment Epping was wishing that he was anywhere but on the train. He was a balding, portly middle-aged man. He considered himself a respectable citizen. He was a regular churchgoer.

He lived in New York, which was largely a respectable city. He was a man who spent all his working life behind a desk. His office was a second home. It was almost an extension of his pleasant house in a reasonably fashionable part of New York. When he left his home in the morning and took the tram to his office he might as well have been going from one room to another in his house. He wasn't a traveller. Travelling by train was anathema to him. Yet, here he was. On a train which was going to be attacked by outlaws at any moment.

It was all his fault. If he hadn't been

so conscientious none of this would have happened. If he hadn't reported to headquarters that he had seen the article in the *New York Argus* he wouldn't be on this train now.

He could have kept quiet. He needn't have reported that he had seen the article in the *New York Argus*. There was no one to say that he had read the newspaper. It wasn't even a newspaper which he habitually took. But lately there had been the running battle between the *Argus* and the banks. It had been compulsive reading, especially at this time of the year when interesting news tended to be rather scarce.

The *Argus* had accused the bank of stifling freedom of speech by refusing to renew their lease. This meant in effect that they would have to close down, or move to an out-of-town location, since the banks also owned most of the suitable business premises in New York. The final shot which the *Argus* had aimed at the bank was to notify the public about the movement of the gold and cash to the West. The article had been dressed up with advice telling people that now was a better time than ever to go West, since the banks there would be receiving large assets with which they could encourage new users. However there was no doubt that the bank managers would have been grinding their teeth at the disclosure that so much money was going West.

The fact that there were a couple of dozen soldiers in the next carriage did offer him some slight comfort. He would assume that the soldiers would be able to deal with any small gang. What, however, if the gang turned out to be a large one? Would the soldiers be able to cope with them then? And what about innocent civilians? There were not only men but a large number of women on the train. He had watched anxiously as they had boarded the train in Chicago. Some had been running to catch the train. If only they had realized that they were dashing to catch a train which was almost certainly going to be attacked by outlaws, they would have let the train go.

A couple of hours later there was an almighty explosion ahead. It was followed by the train giving a sickening lurch.

15

'You let him escape?' Taunton shouted.

'I only just missed him,' said Cowley, defensively. 'My bullet singed his hair.'

'Singed his hair,' snarled his boss. 'What good is that?'

'He dived so quickly off his horse that I didn't have a chance to get him with a second bullet.'

'You're a fool, Cowley. You can't even kill a man at a couple of hundred yards.'

'I'm sure I'll get him next time,' said his repentant foreman.

'There won't be a next time,' growled Taunton. 'You're fired.'

'What?' Cowley stared at his boss with disbelief written on his face. 'You're firing me?'

'That's right. I don't want an inefficient foreman working for me,' said Taunton, calmly.

'You're firing me after all the years' service I've given you?' Cowley was shouting now. 'After all the sweat and hard work. After obeying all your orders. You're firing me just because I missed with one lousy shot?'

'It wasn't just one shot you missed. It was a chance to get rid of Stiles once and for all and to take over his ranch. I've been planning for this for years. Here was our chance. Everything was set up. We had an innocent stranger who we could kill without anyone being concerned about him. All you had to do was to shoot him. And you missed.'

'You're mad,' stormed Cowley. 'Do you know that? And I must have been mad to go along with your plan.'

'You went along with it because of your greed,' sneered Taunton. 'You couldn't resist the temptation of having Stiles's ranch.'

'I don't suppose you would have let me have the ranch if I had managed to kill McGee,' said Cowley, bitterly.

'How clever of you to work that out,'

sneered Taunton.

'Well at least you'll never get Stiles's ranch now,' said Cowley, with more than a hint of triumph in his voice. 'All I have to do is to go to Stiles and tell him that you were behind my attempt to start a range war between the two of you. He'll never let you have his ranch in a hundred years.'

Cowley was standing in front of Taunton who was seated at his desk. The shouting match was taking place in the library which was at the back of the rambling ranch house.

'You don't think he'll believe you, do you?' demanded Taunton, scornfully. 'Now get out,' he hurled the words at his ex-foreman.

'Not before you pay me the wages you owe me,' said Cowley, stubbornly.

Taunton opened a drawer in the desk. There were several piles of hundred-dollar notes in it. He picked out a few of the piles.

'Here,' he deliberately tossed the piles on to the floor.

'You *are* mad,' asserted Cowley, as he bent down to pick up the money. 'I'd always suspected it, but now I know it for a fact. You won't get away with this, you know.'

'Oh, yes I will,' said Taunton.

While his ex-foreman had been collecting the money from the floor, Taunton had produced a revolver from another of the drawers of the desk. When Cowley straightened up he shot him at point-blank range.

★ ★ ★

'He shot at me,' asserted McGee. 'The bullet parted my hair. Look,' he pointed out the trajectory of the bullet to Salmon.

Salmon examined the head in question. 'Now you've got two partings instead of one,' he said.

'I don't think it's funny,' said McGee. 'I'm not staying on this ranch any longer.'

'You're right. Maybe we should move on,' stated Salmon. 'I wouldn't want a father-to-be getting killed.'

'I wonder why he shot at me?' McGee asked himself the question as they rode slowly back to the ranch.

'Maybe he didn't like your face,' suggested Salmon.

'Or maybe he wanted to get even with Taunton about something or other which had happened between them,' said McGee, thoughtfully.

'Who are you talking about?' demanded Salmon.

'Why, Stiles of course.'

They were now nearing the ranch house. A shot rang out. It came from inside the house. They instinctively jumped from their horses and rushed into the house.

They discovered Taunton standing near the body of his foreman.

'He was cleaning some guns,' he explained. 'One of them had a bullet left inside. It went off. I'm afraid he's dead.'

16

On the train there was pandemonium. Men cursed, women screamed, children cried and above all there were the terrible sounds of breaking glass, cracking wood and crunching metals. The train was still moving slowly although it had been stopped by the first explosion. It was now slowly but inexorably toppling over on to its side. People struggled to get out. Some, who were near the door, succeeded in getting out quickly and were helping other passengers to escape. The majority, however, were still trapped inside. Many were bleeding, some had broken limbs and some just lay inert — they were either unconscious or dead. The noise was deafening. The incessant screams were punctuated by groans. Some people were sobbing, a few screamed hysterically, but the worst sound of all was the occasional death rattle as another passenger breathed their last. Then above the sounds of the injured and dying came the unmistakable sound of rifle-fire.

'Somebody's shooting at us,' exclaimed an old man.

For a moment the screams on the train seemed to stop in face of the new terrible noise. The silence only lasted for a few seconds. But it was long enough to verify that the old man was correct.

A young man, who had paused in the act of smashing a window in order to provide an escape route for the occupants of the carriage confirmed it. 'There are some men outside who are firing at us,' he yelled.

'They can't be firing at us,' shouted the old man. 'They must be firing at the soldiers.'

'Perhaps they're bandits,' suggested a young woman.

The train now seemed to have stopped moving. If they could have gone outside they would have seen that of the five carriages on the train the front two had completely left the track and were lying at an obscene angle away from the torn track. Their carriage was balanced in the air at an unnatural angle and looked as though any sudden movement inside it would send it toppling over to join them. The last two carriages were largely intact. The soldiers were returning the fire from the last carriage but one.

'We didn't get the soldiers,' shouted Quail. 'Most of them are still alive.'

'I'll smoke them out,' said Ablet. 'Give me some cover.'

The gang obediently fired at the carriage holding the soldiers. Ablet raced between the fortunate passengers who had so far managed to escape from the train. He bumped into some of them who were staggering around in a daze. He impatiently brushed them aside in his effort to reach the carriage containing the soldiers. Some men cursed him as he pushed past them.

His single-mindedness of purpose meant that he was not even aware of them. When he reached the carriage he automatically dived underneath. He took out one of the sticks of dynamite from the pouch on his waist. He lit the fuse and placed it carefully between the railway tracks. He watched anxiously until he was sure that the spark would reach its objective in a few seconds' time. In fact he had twenty seconds from the time he had lit the fuse to the time the dynamite exploded. This was the standard time-fuse used underground when he had worked in the coal-mines. He knew however that even a healthily glowing fuse like the one he had just lit could fail to detonate the dynamite. Somewhere along the line, for some inexplicable reason, it would go out. Which was why he had been trained to always light a second fuse.

He knew the seconds were ticking away. He had automatically counted from the time he had lit the first fuse.

He counted as he had been taught to count in the mines — one and, two and, three and — which would represent three seconds. He struggled to light the second fuse but the first match was blown out by the wind and he had to fumble for another. His count had now reached ten. He still had a couple of seconds to spare, but things were going to be tight. The second fuse lit and his gaze followed it almost hypnotically as he confirmed that it really was established. He was still automatically counting. He had now reached fourteen. He knew he had just enough time to roll away from under the carriage and run hell for leather for the safety of the trees.

Fifteen — sixteen — he rolled from under the track. A large woman was blocking his path. In his hurry to escape he pushed her to one side, knocking her to the ground. A man who was standing near her said, 'How dare you!' He swung a blow at Ablet. The man's fist caught Ablet on the side of the face. Ablet fell to the ground. He was dazed with the force of the blow. He tried to stagger to his feet. Even as he did so he knew it was too late.

17

The two companions were shocked when they saw the body of the dead foreman. They had not had many dealings with him, but to them he had seemed a decent sort of feller. Their shock was changed to surprise by Taunton's next words.

'You'll have to help me to move the body. There's a spare shed in the back.'

'Shouldn't you leave the body here until the sheriff has seen him?' demanded Salmon.

'I've sent one of the cowboys to fetch him. The sheriff won't mind examining him in the shed.'

'Couldn't you just cover him with a blanket and leave him here until the sheriff arrives?' suggested McGee.

'I'm busy working here,' exclaimed Taunton, testily. 'I don't see that it makes any difference if the sheriff examines him here, or in the shed. He shouldn't have got himself shot,' he added.

McGee was examining the body. 'He must have shot himself in the heart,' he stated.

'Listen, boys,' said Taunton, persuasively. 'I know it's not a pleasant task moving the body. But if you do it there's a hundred dollars in it for you.' He produced a pack of hundred-dollar bills and held them up invitingly.

McGee glanced at Salmon. 'We'll move the body,' he announced, positively.

After they had taken the body to the shed McGee and Salmon held a conference in the bunkhouse. It was deserted, since all the cowboys were still on duty out on the range.

'I don't like it.' McGee voiced his concern about the situation.

'Neither do I,' said Salmon. 'What exactly are we talking about?' he added, puzzled.

'Me getting shot at, then Cowley

getting killed. There are too many people with guns around this place.'

'Cowley shot himself,' Salmon pointed out. 'You can hardly blame somebody else for that.'

'We've cleaned our guns hundreds of times before the shows, but we've never shot ourselves. Why?'

'Because we always check our guns first,' replied Salmon, looking pleased with the fact that he had come up with the correct answer.

'So that leaves another possibility,' said McGee, after looking around to make sure that nobody had come into the bunkhouse.

'What's that?' demanded Salmon.

'What do you think?'

'That he didn't check the gun because he was told it was empty,' said Salmon, slowly. 'So he thought there was no need to check it.'

'Exactly.' McGee couldn't have been more pleased than a teacher whose favourite pupil had suddenly grasped Archimedes' Principle.

He looked around again. Satisfied, he continued: 'Suppose the gun was really Taunton's. Suppose also he had told Cowley that the gun was empty and there was no need to check it for bullets. He was the boss so Cowley would have obeyed him. But when he came to cleaning it there was a bullet left in the chamber. He shot himself with it.'

Salmon nodded slowly. 'That's certainly a possibility,' he concurred.

'It's more than a possibility,' said McGee, with some irritation. 'It's a probability.'

Salmon was still digesting the theory. 'Then in that case Taunton made a mistake about the gun being empty.'

'Or he knew that the gun wasn't empty,' said McGee, pointedly.

'Oh, I don't believe that,' said Salmon, emphatically.

'I'm telling you, there's something fishy about it,' stated McGee. 'And there was one other thing.'

'What's that?' Salmon had to put his

head closer to his companion to hear, since he had dropped his voice to a low whisper.

'There weren't any scorch marks on the body. At least I couldn't see any.'

'If there weren't any scorch marks — oh, no, I don't believe that.' Salmon denied the implication vehemently.

'Shh, keep your voice down,' remonstrated McGee.

'You're suggesting,' this time it was Salmon's turn to whisper in a low voice, 'that Taunton killed him.'

'Well I didn't see any scorch marks. You'd expect to see them wouldn't you, if Cowley shot himself at close range?'

'Yes, there should be scorch marks,' said the other, slowly. 'Remember that guy working for the circus who shot himself because his girlfriend was in love with somebody else?'

'Gerrard,' supplied McGee.

'Yes, well we found the body in his tent. There were definitely scorch marks on his shirt. You couldn't miss them.'

'So Taunton could have shot him.' McGee repeated the obvious conclusion.

'Whether he did or not, there's one thing for sure,' said Salmon.

'What's that?' demanded McGee.

'We're not staying here any longer.' He began to pack his few belongings into his bag.

'I think you're right. It's too dangerous.' McGee began to copy him. They were interrupted by the arrival of Taunton.

'Hullo boys,' he greeted them jovially. His expression changed when he saw that they were packing. 'Where do you think you're going?' he snapped.

'We're leaving,' said McGee. 'I was shot at while I was riding the range this afternoon. Now Cowley has been killed. There are too many bullets flying around here.'

'I told you that Cowley was killed in an accident,' said Taunton, irritably. 'The sheriff will confirm it when he arrives.'

'Anyhow, we'll be on our way,' said Salmon.

'I was just coming to offer you boys the job of new foreman,' said Taunton. 'You could share the job between you. You could also share the money. A hundred dollars a week between you.'

'No, thanks,' said Salmon.

'We'll take it,' said McGee.

18

In his office Carter was studying the report of the great train robbery, as it was now being called by the Press. Pike, his assistant, sat in front of the desk. His morose expression mirrored the fact that the news was very bad.

'They've got away with nine hundred thousand dollars,' said Carter, eventually. 'They had to leave some of the gold behind because a few of the gang were killed during the robbery. The ones who were left couldn't carry it all.'

'So if those members of the gang hadn't been killed they would probably have got away with a million dollars,' suggested Pike.

'Probably,' said Carter, casually.

Pike in fact was surprised by Carter's attitude to the whole report. He had expected him to rant and rave as he usually did. But here he was just accepting it as if it were some minor robbery.

'Does it say how many people were killed?' asked Pike.

'No. It will take them some time before they get the final figure. Some of the passengers had their limbs blown off with the explosions and that will make them more difficult to identify.'

'I heard they've brought some of the injured back to the hospitals here,' ventured Pike, still not sure how long his boss's equanimity would continue.

'Yes. Although the robbery actually took place three hundred miles from here, there aren't enough hospitals out there to cope with the injured. So a lot of them are in our hospitals.'

Pike broached the question he had been dying to raise. 'We know it's the work of the Quail gang, so when do we start going after them?' he demanded.

'All in good time,' said Carter, in that infuriatingly casual manner which he had adopted since Pike had come into the room.

The reason for his boss's apparent indifference to the report he had read was revealed soon after when a dishevelled figure was led into the room. He was handcuffed to a policeman.

'I won't ask you to sit,' said Carter, sarcastically addressing the prisoner.

Pike studied him. He was a man in his early thirties. He must have been good-looking once but now he presented a sorry sight. He had a bloody bandage round his head and his left arm was in a sling. It appeared as though it had been broken.

'Your name is Pierre Plouviez,' said Carter, studying a piece of paper on his desk. 'You are a deserter from the army. You go by the nickname of Frenchie. Is that right?'

Frenchie shrugged. At a signal from Carter, the policeman hit him on his damaged arm.

Frenchie screamed.

'There, that was a simple question,' said Carter. 'It would have been easier, and less painful for you to have answered it.'

'I'm Pierre Plouviez,' said the prisoner, sullenly.

'And you are one of the Quail gang,' said Carter, conversationally.

'Since you've got it written down in front of you there's no point in denying it,' muttered Frenchie.

'Speak up, I can't hear you,' said Carter.

Frenchie repeated his statement.

'Now,' said Carter, consulting his document, 'I suppose you know that three of the gang were killed in the robbery by the soldiers. Their names are Cooper, Watson and Glasebury.' It was obvious from Frenchie's expression that he hadn't known that. 'So how many does that leave alive?'

For a moment it appeared that Frenchie was not going to answer the question, but when the policeman raised his arm again threateningly he relented. 'Nine,' he replied.

'One of the gang was blown up under

the train. So there were fourteen in the gang,' said Carter, thoughtfully.

'That's right.'

'Now you're going to give me their names and descriptions,' said Carter.

'What if I refuse,' said Frenchie, showing the first glimmer of aggression he had shown since entering the room.

'Then I will hand you back to the army authorities,' said Carter. 'You will be court-martialled again and undoubtedly shot.'

'What if I agree to co-operate,' demanded Frenchie, with a crafty smile.

'You will go to jail. You will be kept there until your trial. At your trial I will confirm that you have helped with our inquiries. It could get your sentence reduced.'

'At least it's better than being shot at dawn,' said Frenchie, with a philosophical shrug. 'What do you want to know?'

19

The day of the rodeo eventually arrived. The previous week had been uneventful. After Cowley's death, for which the sheriff accepted Taunton's explanation without questioning it, McGee and Salmon had gone about their daily tasks rather uneasily, especially McGee. Taunton had suggested that they should ride keeping close together.

'That way the Stiles boys will think twice about attacking you when they see that there are two of you,' Taunton pointed out.

They had obeyed his instructions. Even so McGee kept looking over his shoulder as they rode around the range searching for any stray steers.

'Your head will twist off if you keep on turning it like that,' observed Salmon.

'Your head will be sore after I hit it if you make any more stupid remarks like that,' retorted McGee.

Although it had been originally intended that McGee would be practising his riding skills in preparation for the rodeo, in fact he was denied any practice before the event. The death of Cowley, his subsequent funeral, the fact that the duo had been officially given the position of foremen, all meant that the rodeo had become a minor event.

McGee did, however, broach the subject with Taunton. He entered Taunton's study one evening. His boss greeted him with a welcoming smile and the offer of a cigar. McGee accepted the cigar.

He couldn't help glancing at the carpet where Cowley's body had been lying a few days before.

'I've come to see whether there are any special instructions about the rodeo,' he ventured.

'Just stay on the horse,' said Taunton, with a smile.

'How many seconds will I have to do it for?'

'Last year Stiles's rider stayed on for eight seconds. He managed to win,' said Taunton, bitterly.

'I suppose there will be some bets going on the contest,' said McGee, thoughtfully.

'The last time I heard the odds they were five to one against you,' stated Taunton.

Later McGee broached the subject of the bets with Salmon.

'I could make a thousand dollars for just staying on the horse for about ten seconds,' he told him.

'I thought the prize money was only two hundred dollars,' replied Salmon, suspiciously.

'That's right, but the rest of the money will be our winnings when you put a bet on.'

'Your loss you mean. I'm having nothing to do with it,' retorted Salmon.

'We can rustle a couple of hundred dollars together between us,' said

McGee, ignoring Salmon's objection.

'I'm not betting my hard-earned money on you falling off a horse,' Salmon announced decisively.

'I've only got to stay on for ten seconds,' pleaded McGee. 'Anyhow what's all this about hard-earned money? We've never had an easier job. Nor a better-paid one either, thanks to me.'

'What do you mean, thanks to you?'

'Well if I hadn't got shot at in the first place you wouldn't be a foreman now.'

'I don't think you can claim any credit for being shot at,' said Salmon drily.

In the end McGee persuaded him to put all the money they had on him winning the rodeo. It amounted to two hundred dollars.

'At five to one we'll make a thousand dollars on the bet,' said McGee, happily.

'You'd better stay on that horse,' growled Salmon. 'Or I'll see that your backside is so sore that you won't be able to sit down for a week.'

'It'll be a cinch,' said McGee.

He changed his mind though when he saw the black stallion named Demon which he would have to ride. It took half a dozen cowboys to saddle him in the enclosure where he was being held. He managed to lay two of them out with well-aimed kicks.

'He does seem to have plenty of energy,' said McGee, thoughtfully.

A small group of cowboys were watching Demon's frenzied movements from the other side of the enclosure. One of them came over to McGee.

'I'd better introduce myself,' he drawled. 'My name is Lunt. I'm the one who's going to win on Demon this afternoon.' He was a handsome blond cowboy. He held out his hand invitingly towards McGee.

'You'll excuse me if I don't shake hands with you,' snapped McGee. 'I don't shake hands with a man from an outfit who has taken a shot at me.'

Lunt flushed. 'I don't know what

you're talking about,' he said.

McGee gussed from Lunt's expression that he was lying. He turned on his heel and joined Salmon and the other Lazy Y cowboys.

'That wasn't a very polite thing to do,' observed Salmon. 'After all he did offer to shake hands with you.'

'I accused him of working for an outfit who took a pot shot at me,' explained McGee. 'He denied it, but I could tell that he was lying,' he added, tautly.

'Those Tall T cowboys are getting too big for their boots,' said Jones.

Salmon noticed that all his friends were wearing guns. Normally Taunton wouldn't allow them to wear guns. Of course they were off duty now and therefore they could do what they liked. He also noticed that Stiles cowboys on the other side of the enclosure were wearing their guns. Was there any significance in this? Or did they just wear them to a rodeo as part of their normal dress? He glanced around. He also noticed something else — none of the other townsfolk and cowboys from other ranches were wearing their guns.

He wondered whether to bring his observations to McGee's notice. But McGee seemed to be in a trance as he stood by the enclosure. Salmon had seen him like this one a few occasions before. On one of them McGee had believed that a certain member of the circus troupe had been making eyes at Letitia. When McGee had accused him of the reprehensible deed, the man had replied, 'So what?'

It had obviously been the wrong answer since McGee had challenged him to a fight. The man, a big Swede named Svenson, had accepted with alacrity. He was a head taller than McGee and a couple of stones heavier. However McGee had set about him like a tiger. In no time he had hit Svenson down. When the Swede, in a dazed state, had shown that he was in no hurry to get up, McGee had pounded his head as he lay on the floor. Salmon had to pick him up bodily and carry him away from the unfortunate Swede.

McGee had the same glazed expression on his face now as he had had that afternoon. Salmon decided that now was not the right time to interrupt his thoughts. He walked quickly away to the enclosure where they had tied up their horses. He asked one of the cowboys on duty when the rodeo would start.

'In about ten minutes' time,' replied the cowboy.

As Salmon jumped on his horse he knew he wouldn't be able to ride to the ranch and back in ten minutes. But he also knew that what he was going to fetch was of vital importance. He was going to get his guns and McGee's guns. Because he had seen from the expressions on the faces on the rival cowboys that they were looking for trouble. When it came he wanted to make sure that they too had their guns with them.

20

In a lonely valley a few hundred miles west of Chicago nine members of the Quail gang were sharing out their loot.

'There's enough here to keep us in luxury for the rest of our lives,' said Quail, delightedly.

'It's a pity that the others won't be able to share the money,' said Hislop.

'It means more money for the rest of us,' said Lille, amid general laughter.

'Anyhow apart from the three who were shot by the soldiers, Ablet and Frenchie are missing,' Quail reminded the remaining members of the gang.

'I saw Ablet trying to escape before the carriage blew up.' The contribution to the discussion came from the youngest member of the gang, a youth named Ringer. 'It was horrible the way he was hit down by that man when he was trying to get away. After that he was just blown up by his own dynamite.'

'What about Frenchie?' demanded Cleeves, another soldier who had deserted from the army. 'They've captured him. I saw the soldiers dragging him away.'

'Yes, it's a pity they've got Frenchie,' said Quail, thoughtfully.

'The Pinkerton Agency would probably have got our descriptions from him,' said Hislop.

'You mean the authorities will know who we are?' demanded a shocked Ringer.

'What do you expect?' said Lille, scornfully.

'Maybe Frenchie won't talk,' suggested Cleeves.

'Don't be stupid,' stated Quail. 'Of course he'll talk. They'll threaten to send him back to the army if he doesn't. That way he'll definitely get shot.'

'The way you'd get shot if they captured you,' stated a Mexican named Ricardo.

Cleeves, who was on a short fuse, flared up. 'I'll get you, you bastard,' he snarled. 'Then there'll be one less to share the money out.'

'All right, that'll be enough.' Quail was forced to shout to try to keep order.

'How long do you think it will be before the authorities get our pictures?' demanded a worried Ringer.

'They've probably got them by now. But they'll have to send them around the territories,' said Hislop. 'That should take some time.'

'Yes, it will, won't it,' said a slightly relieved Ringer.

'Anyhow, you'll be all right,' said Stan, one of a pair of brothers named Bryce. 'You can always grow a moustache. The authorities won't recognize you then.'

'He's been trying to grow one for ages,' said his brother, Frank.

There was general laughter. Quail was relieved that the tone of the meeting had become more light-hearted.

'Anyhow, it's true, we've got to think about where we're going next,' he said.

'What about San Francisco?' said a

small thin Irishman named Murphy. 'I hear it's called Sin City. I could do with some sinning after what we've been through.'

'You're free to go if you want to,' said Quail. 'In fact everyone is free to leave now if you want to.'

Nobody showed any sign of moving off.

'Where do you think we should head for?' demanded Lille.

'Well, I think it will take some time before the authorities get our descriptions out to the towns in the West. There are too many of them for one thing. They'll have to send the posters out by stagecoach to some of them. So I think we've got a couple of weeks at least while we can enjoy ourselves.'

'Sounds all right to me,' said Murphy, rubbing his hands.

'After that, if you don't want to end up in jail, we'll head for the Canadian border. Once we're in Canada we'll be safe from the authorities. We can spend our money as we like.'

There was general acceptance of his plan. The only objector was Ricardo.

'I agree with spending the next few weeks on wine, women and song,' he stated. 'But I don't fancy going to Canada. They have snow up there. When we've finished enjoying ourselves I'll head down south for Mexico. It's a lot warmer there.'

'If the authorities catch up with you and you get shot, where you'll end up will be hotter still,' said Frank Bryce.

There was general laughter. Quail regarded the company benignly. He was proud of his gang of outlaws. They had pulled off one of the most daring train-raids in the history of the United States. True, quite a number of innocent people had been killed. But that was the luck of the draw. He knew that if they were caught by the law they would be summarily hanged. That, too, was the luck of the draw. In the meantime they were going to move west and stop at the most suitable town they came to.

21

McGee was impatiently watching the display of steer-roping which was a preliminary to the main event, the riding of Demon. From time to time he kept glancing around, trying to find Salmon's face among the crowd.

Taunton came over to him. 'Feeling nervous?' he demanded.

'Not particularly. I usually feel relaxed when I'm waiting to go on to do my act in the circus.'

'Well, make sure you win. I've got a few dollars resting on you.' Taunton gave McGee a friendly pat on the shoulder before going back to his reserved seat above the enclosure.

Jones materialized by his side. 'What do you think are your chances?' he demanded.

McGee answered with a question of his own. 'Have you seen Salmon?'

'I think he went back to the ranch. Well, do you think you'll win?'

'Of course I'll win,' stated McGee. 'I'll beat that smug Swede if it's the last thing I do.'

'That's the spirit,' said Jones, patting him on the back.

The master of ceremonies declared that the steer-roping was over. He added that there would be a short interval before the main event: the competition to see who could stay on a horse the longest. The announcement brought a cheer from the rival camps. McGee noticed that the Stiles camp were more vociferous than his own supporters.

The master of ceremonies came over to him.

'Are you ready?' he demanded.

McGee gave one despairing glance around. There was still no sign of Salmon. 'As ready as I'll ever be,' he confirmed.

'Ladies and gentlemen.' The master of ceremonies began his announcement. 'The next item is the main one of the afternoon. It is a contest to see who can stay on a horse the longest. There will be three bouts. The winner will be the one who wins two out of the three.'

This was news to McGee who had assumed that there would be one bout and the winner would be crowned the undisputed champion. Well, it wouldn't make any difference. One bout or three.

'Since you are the challenger,' the MC addressed the remark to McGee, 'you've got the choice of going first or last.'

McGee's reply was delayed by the arrival of Salmon.

'Where have you been?' he growled.

'I've been getting our guns,' replied his companion.

'I'm going to ride the horse, not shoot him,' replied McGee.

'I'll tell you later,' said Salmon.

The moment of truth had arrived. McGee mounted Demon assisted by Salmon and Jones. An expectant hush descended on the crowd. The gate was opened. Demon hurled himself into the enclosure with the stranger on his back. The crowd began to count. 'One — two . . .'

They got no further since, with an acrobatic jump and convulsive turn, Demon tossed McGee from the saddle. He landed on the ground with a thud.

'You're supposed to stay on him,' said Salmon, as he helped his friend to his feet. He saw from McGee's scowl that it wasn't the time for flippant remarks.

McGee's expression was intensified when Lunt mounted the horse. The crowd began to count. They reached six before he was eventually thrown. As he got up and dusted himself down he flashed a triumphant smile towards McGee.

Salmon had been helping to catch the rampant Demon — who was already doing a victory jig around the enclosure. When everything was again ready he advised McGee, 'Stay on longer this time.'

To the surprise of the spectators,

McGee did stay on longer that time. The crowd had reached the count of seven before Demon finally tossed the troublesome burden from his back.

Lunt mounted Demon. The smile of triumph was no longer on his face. It was reflected in his performance. He bit the dust at the count of four.

'This will be the deciding bout,' the master of ceremonies told the spectators.

'If you can make it to seven, you'll beat him,' advised Salmon.

To everyone's surprise McGee made it to nine. His companions from the Lazy Y ranch whistled and cheered when he was finally unseated. This time McGee flashed a triumphant smile at Lunt.

The smile was justified. Demon, as though growing weary of the game, reared and twisted in one convulsive movement. It would have unseated any rider. It had that effect on Lunt. He hit the dust before the crowd had reached two.

McGee stepped forward to receive his prize money. His face wore a satisfied smile. The Lazy Y cowboys whistled and cheered. Taunton's face wore the widest smile Salmon had seen. As he glanced around he noticed something else. A Tall T cowboy had drawn his revolver and was aiming it at McGee. Salmon didn't hesitate. He drew his own gun with lightning speed and shot the cowboy. It was a signal for all hell to be let loose.

22

The range war between the Lazy Y ranch and the Tall T went on for several days. After the initial shoot-out at the rodeo both factions had retired to their respective ranches to lick their wounds and assess the situation. In spite of the fact that there had been considerable gunfire, since the cowboys were not trained gunslingers, there were surprisingly few casualties. The cowboy whom Salmon had aimed at was fortunate in that he had only a shattered hand to testify to his rash action in pulling a gun on McGee.

'That was a good shot,' said McGee, appreciatively.

'Haven't you got anything else to say?' demanded Salmon.

'Yes, well, thanks for saving my life,' confessed McGee.

'Now we can go ahead with our

original plan,' said Salmon.

'What's that?' demanded McGee.

'Why, to get the hell out of here. We don't want to get mixed up in a range war,' said Salmon, positively.

'Taunton has offered us a bonus of a thousand dollars between us if we see this thing through,' said McGee, persuasively.

'The answer is no,' said Salmon. 'Anyhow it won't be any good to us if we're dead.'

'There's no danger of that,' said McGee. 'You saw the cowboys at the rodeo. They can't shoot. They couldn't hit a barn door at ten paces.'

'The answer is still no,' said Salmon. 'You could get one cowboy with one lucky shot who could send us to Kingdom Come.'

'We've got a thousand dollars,' said McGee. 'If we get an extra thousand we can write to the girls and ask them to come here. We'd have enough money to settle down. You'd like that, wouldn't you?'

Salmon wavered. 'You promise that we'd get in touch with the girls if we get the extra thousand?'

'Cross my heart and hope to die,' said McGee.

Ten minutes later they informed Taunton that they would accept his offer.

'Thanks, boys,' he said, enthusiastically. 'You won't regret this. I want to wipe Stiles off the face of the earth once and for all. With your help I'm sure I'll be able to do it.'

'He doesn't seem to like Stiles,' observed Salmon, when they were back in their cabin. They had been allocated the log cabin on the demise of Cowley. It had once been his. They had stacked his belongings neatly in a corner.

'As long as he pays us our thousand dollars, he can dislike the president as far as I'm concerned,' said McGee.

Later the same day one of the cowboys knocked at the cabin door.

'There's someone to collect Cowley's belongings,' he announced.

The someone turned out to be a very pretty young lady. She was a blonde with the perfect complexion that some of them have. When she came in she looked around.

'I see you couldn't wait to take over my father's room,' she said, icily.

'I didn't know he was your father,' said McGee.

'We're only obeying instructions,' Salmon pointed out.

She stared at the pile of garments and guns in the corner. 'Is that all?' she demanded.

'Yes,' said McGee. 'That's all.'

'Have you got a buggy?' asked Salmon.

'Yes.' She was still staring at the pile of belongings. Her confidence had evaporated. She seemed unable to move.

'I'll help you to carry them out,' said Salmon, gently.

'Thanks, I can manage,' she said, stiffly.

She picked up an armful. Salmon opened the door for her. At that moment there came the sound of a shot. Salmon pushed her back into the cabin.

McGee had grabbed a rifle and now peered round the open door. He was greeted by another bullet. It embedded itself in the woodwork above his head.

'Cover me,' he instructed Salmon.

'Where did the shots come from?'

'Somewhere on the right,' came the answer.

Salmon took up his position by the door.

'Now!' yelled McGee.

Salmon let loose a volley from his Winchester. The gunman outside replied with a solitary shot. Before he followed it with another McGee had dived out through the door. He moved with lightning speed, eventually taking cover behind a water trough.

He cautiously poked his head above the trough. He was greeted with a couple of bullets, neither of which found its target. However, in the split second when he had put his head up McGee had seen the flash of the rifle. He now knew where the gunman was hiding.

He was behind a deserted old barn which stood about a hundred yards from the ranch. McGee looked around for some way to get the rifleman to come out of hiding. He eventually hit on an idea.

The buggy that the young lady had arrived in was situated to McGee's right. He signalled to Salmon who was still standing concealed behind the open door. The signal meant 'cover me'.

Salmon did just that. McGee raced for the buggy. He reached it before the rifleman put his head round the corner of the barn.

McGee yelled at the horse in the buggy. It was already in a nervous state brought on by the close proximity of the bullets whistling above its head. On hearing McGee's shouts it needed no second bidding. It took off as though it were in the Kentucky Derby.

McGee clung to the side of the buggy as the horse hared towards the open ground. When McGee judged that he was far enough away from the barn he jumped off the buggy. He was greeted by a bullet. It was too far away to do any damage.

The gunman, who until now had held the upper hand, suddenly realized that he was caught in crossfire. Salmon was shooting at him from the cabin, while McGee was now to the right of the barn and so he had no cover in that direction.

He decided to make a run for it. His horse was a hundred or so yards behind him. He fired a couple of shots in McGee's direction. He jumped out from behind the barn and started to run towards his horse. McGee took careful aim and fired.

Ten minutes later McGee was bringing the cowboy back to the cabin. He had retrieved the buggy and had placed the cowboy's body inside. As he approached the barn the woman ran out.

'You've killed him,' she said, accusingly.

McGee was surprised by her reaction.

'I've shot him in the leg,' he explained. 'He won't be going to any dances for a while.'

If McGee was surprised by the young lady's reaction, he was even more surprised by the cowboy's next words.

'I'm sorry, Mrs Stiles,' he replied. 'I seem to have made a mess of things.'

23

McGee and Salmon were disgesting their visitor's remark while she was bandaging the leg of the unfortunate cowboy. He was howling with pain as she washed the wound.

'Serves you right,' she snapped. 'You shouldn't be going around shooting at people.'

'I never intended to kill anybody,' he whined.

'Nor me,' said McGee, pleasantly. 'So we're quits.'

'Who told you to come here and start shooting?' she demanded.

'Your father-in-law,' came the reply.

This time light dawned on McGee and Salmon. 'Then old Mr Stiles isn't your husband?' Salmon demanded.

For the first time she smiled. 'Don't be stupid,' she said. 'I'm married to Adam, his son.'

'And Mr Cowley was your father?' confirmed Salmon.

'That's right. He quarrelled with my father-in-law. That was why he was here working for the madman, Taunton,' she said, bitterly.

'Why do you call him a madman?' demanded McGee.

'Because he is. He's like two different persons. One minute he's all smiles, the next he can change into a raving lunatic. My father used to tell me about him. But you won't want to hear about that, since you're working for him. There.' She addressed the last remark to the cowboy whose leg she had now finished binding.

'If you can tell us anything about Taunton, we'd like to know,' said McGee, earnestly. 'We don't want to get involved in any gunfights if he's the cause.'

'That's right, we're just passing through,' affirmed Salmon.

She surveyed them for a few moments as though gauging in her mind whether she could trust them. At last she came to a conclusion.

'He killed my father,' she said, baldly.

'Hang on, that's quite an accusation to make,' said Salmon.

'I knew you wouldn't believe me,' she said, as she turned and headed for the door.

'Have you got any proof of that?' asked McGee.

'Only what the deputy sheriff told me,' she stated.

'And what did the deputy sheriff tell you?' asked Salmon.

'It's no good.' She turned to leave. 'You won't believe me.'

'It was about the fact that there were no scorch marks on the body wasn't it?' demanded McGee.

She turned to face him. 'How did you know?'

'We got here a few minutes after he was shot,' McGee explained. 'We saw the body.'

'We helped to move him,' chipped in Salmon.

'Why is the deputy sheriff involved in this and not the sheriff?' demanded McGee.

'The sheriff is in Taunton's pay,' she said bitterly. 'He always has been. That's why he has got away with stealing our cattle over the years. And trying to start a range war so that he could take over our ranch.'

'I thought your outfit were the ones who were stealing the cattle,' said Salmon.

'Taunton was behind it. I can confirm that,' said the cowboy. He had found a chair to sit on and had been listening to the discussion with interest.

'If you want further proof go to see the deputy sheriff. The sheriff is away so Danny will be in his office on his own.'

'We'd like to get the truth confirmed,' said McGee.

Mrs Stiles set off back towards her ranch with the wounded cowboy in the buggy. He gave McGee and Salmon a friendly wave before setting out.

'No hard feelings,' he told McGee.

The duo saddled their horses and rode the couple of miles into town. They drew up outside the sheriff's office. They went inside and introduced themselves to Danny.

McGee explained the purpose of their visit. While he was doing so Salmon glanced idly at the drawings of the Wanted criminals which were spaced around the wall.

'It's my opinion that Mr Cowley was shot by someone who was standing at least a couple of feet away,' said Danny. He was a ginger-haired middle-aged man with a freckled face. 'Otherwise there would have been scorch marks. But there's nothing I can do about it. The sheriff was in charge. The body has been buried, anyhow.'

'Thanks for telling us,' said McGee. 'It confirmed what I'd already guessed.'

He turned to leave. Salmon was still studying the drawings on the wall.

'They just came in today,' explained Danny. 'They're members of a gang who held up a train outside Chicago about ten days ago. They're known as the Quail gang.'

24

McGee and Salmon were arguing as they rode out of Stoneville.

'It's none of our business,' said Salmon, stubbornly.

'We're getting paid fifty dollars each,' McGee reminded him. 'I want to know what we're getting into.'

'We just keep our heads down and we'll be all right,' said Salmon.

'That's what Cowley thought and look what happened to him,' said McGee.

'Yes, you might have a point there,' Salmon conceded after giving the matter some thought.

'So we're going to find out a bit more about this range war,' stated McGee. 'If Taunton is as mad as Mrs Stiles says he is, then we'll have to think about moving on.'

'How do you intend finding out

whether Taunton is mad or not? Are you going to ask him?' demanded Salmon, sarcastically.

'No, I want a few more facts,' said McGee. 'That's why we're going to ride out to Stiles's ranch.'

'Are you sure that's a good idea?' said a worried Salmon. 'The last time we rode near the ranch they shot at you.'

'I don't think they'll shoot at us this time,' said McGee. 'Mrs Stiles should have put the word out that we're not gunslingers. Just two harmless fellers who are passing through.'

In fact they made it to the Stiles ranch safely, although two of their cowboys joined them at a safe distance and rode in with them.

The Stiles ranch was on a smaller scale than Taunton's. Apart from the two cowboys who had intercepted them there was no sign of life as they tied their horses to the hitching rail.

Mrs Stiles came out to meet them. She greeted them with a friendly smile.

'You're just in time for afternoon tea,'

she said. 'It's a habit I picked up when I used to live in Boston.'

'We're from New York,' volunteered Salmon. 'Lots of people used to take afternoon tea there.'

Tea was served out on the veranda. They were joined by a grey-haired man with a weatherbeaten face. 'This is my father-in-law,' said Mrs Stiles.

He regarded the two men suspiciously. 'I don't normally have any truck with cowboys from Taunton's ranch,' he stated, uncompromisingly.

'We're only working for Taunton temporarily,' explained McGee. 'We're just trying to find out the truth about what he's been up to.'

'I'll tell you what he's been up to.' Stiles stood up and thumped the table. 'He's been trying to take over my ranch for the past ten years. He's harassed my cowboys, stolen my stock and made our lives a misery. He's even hired gunslingers from time to time, like you two,' he concluded, bitterly.

'We're not gunslingers. We used to

work in a circus,' explained Salmon.

'Then what are you doing working for Taunton?' Stiles was still suspicious.

'It's a long story,' said McGee. 'What we're trying to do is to find out whether Taunton is as mad as your daughter-in-law says he is.'

'He shot her father. That's proof enough,' snapped Stiles.

'We went into town and saw the deputy sheriff.' McGee addressed his remark to Mrs Stiles. He had seen that he was not going to get anywhere in trying to reason with the old man. 'He confirmed what I'd noticed — that there were no scorch marks on your father's shirt.'

'I know. But Taunton will get away with it. He always does,' she said, bitterly.

'You said the sheriff is away,' said McGee, thoughtfully.

'That's right,' she confirmed. 'He's away in Canada. He always goes there for a couple of weeks about this time of the year.'

'Then perhaps now is the time to act,' said McGee.

'Hang on. We're not getting mixed up in this. It's not our battle,' said Salmon, with some heat.

'No, it's not your battle,' she said. 'He shot my father. We'll never get justice out here.'

'Thanks for the tea,' said McGee, as he stood up.

Salmon followed his example, only more slowly. As they rode away from the Stiles ranch he demanded: 'What are we going to do next?'

'We're going to have a showdown with Taunton,' McGee announced.

'Oh, no we're not,' stated Salmon, positively. 'As the lady said, it's not our battle.'

'If we don't bring him to justice, who will?' retorted McGee. 'We're the only ones in a position to see that justice is done. Nobody else can do anything about it except us. So we've got to accept our responsibility.'

'What's all this about responsibility?'

demanded Salmon. 'You've never wanted any responsibility before.'

'Yes, well maybe I see things differently out here.' McGee waved a dramatic arm taking in the lush wide valley with its cattle scattered all over it.

'You're as mad as Taunton,' said Salmon, disconsolately.

'Maybe you'll change your mind one day, too,' said McGee.

25

In Chicago Letitia and Jill were helping Daley to refurbish the opera house. Letitia was still hobbling around with the aid of a stick. She had twisted her ankle while the two had been running for the train, as Jill had reminded her a hundred times since.

'If you hadn't twisted your ankle we'd have caught the train and we'd have been blown up with the rest of those people.'

Daley had been standing on the platform waiting for them to get on the train. When he had seen Letitia fall he had hurriedly grabbed their cases and dived off the train before it had gathered speed.

When he had reached the prostrate Letitia he had been relieved to find that her fall was not too serious. He took charge of the situation.

'If your friend will hire a buggy, I'll help you to reach it,' he said.

'Where are we going?' demanded Letitia, as she made her painful progress by hanging on to him.

'There won't be another train today. You two can stay in the opera house. There are plenty of dressing-rooms there which you can use. I'll be staying there myself. I'll be starting renovating the place tomorrow.'

So they stayed the first night in the opera house. Daley put them in the two dressing-rooms which the stars would have occupied. They were quite large rooms with comfortable couches on which they could sleep.

'This beats sleeping in a tent,' observed Jill, when she first examined her accommodation.

'It's all right for you,' grumbled Letitia. 'You'll be able to walk around. Daley said I'll have to lie down on this couch until the swelling goes down.'

Daley was secretly pleased to have their company for a few days. There were only a few workmen in the opera house and he found that the two were excellent company and when he wasn't working he would join them for coffee.

Their usual topic of conversation was the robbery. He would buy an early morning paper and they would eagerly scan it for news about the tragedy. The business of recovering the bodies was slow, but each day there would be a few additional bodies discovered.

One day Daley announced: 'There are forty-six dead to date.'

'Oh, how horrible,' exclaimed Jill.

'Let's hope they catch the bastards who did it,' stated Jill.

'They say here,' Daley tapped the paper, 'that it was the work of the Quail gang. There's a reward of a thousand dollars for each of the gang who is still alive.'

'So some had their just deserts,' observed Jill.

'It seems so. Particularly the one who blew up the carriage in the end. He went up with it.'

'Can't we talk about something more pleasant,' complained Letitia. 'I'm sure the baby in here,' she patted her stomach, 'knows what we're talking about. He makes me feel ill when we're discussing the tragedy on the train.'

'If you're still feeling ill from time to time perhaps you should stay here a few days longer,' suggested Daley.

'I think it would be better,' concurred Jill.

'It's all right for you,' stated Letitia, when Daley had gone back to his work. 'You can get around. You can help Daley with the curtains and décor. I've got to stay here like a lemon.'

'You've got books to read,' Jill replied soothingly. 'I can see you've almost finished the last one that Daley brought you.'

'I didn't think much of it,' said Letitia. 'It's by an English author named Jane Austen. It's called *Pride and Prejudice*. I don't think it will ever become popular.'

Jill broached the subject that was

worrying her. 'I haven't heard from Salmon,' she stated.

'How many days ago was it when you sent him the last telegram?'

'I sent him a telegram before we set off from New York. I told him that we coming to join them. I also told him that you were pregnant. Then I sent him a telegram the day after we came here. I told him where we were staying.'

'Then that's probably it,' said Letitia. 'The boys are on their way to join us. It will take them a few days to get here. Especially if they're travelling in their usual way by jumping trains.'

26

'So what are you going to do?' demanded Salmon, scornfully. 'Go into Taunton's study and say 'Mr Taunton I know you're a murderer. I know you killed Cowley. Why don't you come along with me to see the deputy sheriff and we arrange for you to get hung'.'

'Hanged,' corrected McGee.

'Well, whatever, it's all the same in the end. It's a stupid idea.'

'We can't just walk away from it as though it never happened,' said McGee, stubbornly.

'I can. Well at least I can ride away. Just watch me.'

The two were so busy arguing that they did not notice that there was a change from the usual peacefulness of the ranch at this hour. Cowboys were hanging around outside. Normally these cowboys would have been inside the bunkhouse. Possibly playing cards, or writing a letter or in some cases reading a book. To cowboys who had spent hours on the range, the cool of the bunkhouse was a welcome haven. And they always took advantage of it before they had their evening chow.

McGee and Salmon had almost reached the ranch before they both noticed the change to the usual situation. At least a dozen cowboys were hanging around outside. That in itself was odd. What was even more suspicious was the fact that all the cowboys were wearing guns.

McGee called out to Jones, who was standing in front of a small group of men.

'What are you all doing wearing your guns?'

'We're going to ride to the Tall T ranch. We're going to finish the job we should have finished ages ago.'

'You're going to fight a range war?' demanded Salmon, aghast.

'They've been stealing our cattle for

years. They started it,' shouted one of the cowboys.

'Yes!' There was a chorus of agreement from the others.

'Listen, you've got it wrong.' McGee was shouting to get their attention. 'It's not the Tall T who've been stealing our cattle. It was Cowley. He was obeying orders from Taunton. He was trying to take over the Tall T ranch. He's been trying to do so for years.'

'Why should we believe you?' demanded a cowboy from the back. 'The boss has promised us a nice fat bonus if we ride over to the Tall T ranch and take it over.'

'Do you think they're going to let you do it — just like that?' demanded McGee. 'They're going to start shooting when you come within range. Many of you won't be alive to collect that nice fat bonus.'

His words brought some mutterings of discontent. It was obvious that the cowboys hadn't envisaged a prolonged gun-battle.

A figure rode round from the corral. It was Taunton.

'Don't listen to those two,' he shouted. 'They are traitors. They visited the Stiles ranch this afternoon.'

'We were only trying to get at the truth,' said McGee.

'The truth is that you are working hand-in-glove with Stiles. I was a fool ever to have trusted you.'

The mood of the cowboys had suddenly become angry. There were shouts of 'traitors' and 'bastards', and among the other abuse which was being hurled about was the ominous mention of hanging.

'Listen to me.' McGee had to shout at the top of his voice to get himself heard. 'This man,' he pointed at Taunton, 'killed Cowley. He shot him in cold blood and pretended Cowley had accidentally killed himself while cleaning his gun.'

'It's lies. It's all lies,' shouted Taunton.

'There were no scorch marks on

Cowley's shirt,' yelled McGee. 'We moved the body and we can swear to that.'

'If that's the case, why didn't the sheriff take action?' demanded one of the cowboys.

'Because Taunton has got him in his pocket,' said McGee. 'But we've been to see the deputy sheriff and he confirms what we've told you.'

While McGee was speaking Taunton had manoeuvered his horse to the front of the group of cowboys. McGee was busy trying to impress the cowboys with the truth of his statements and hadn't noticed the movement. He did however catch Taunton's next movement out of the corner of his eye.

Three things happened so quickly that they almost appeared to be simultaneous. Taunton, who had sur-reptitiously drawn his gun, fired at McGee. McGee fell from his saddle. Salmon drew his gun with lightning speed and shot Taunton.

27

In Chicago Letitia and Jill were discussing the fact that Salmon hadn't replied to their telegram.

'Maybe he didn't receive it,' said Letitia. 'They say the telegraph service isn't as reliable as all that.'

'He received my first two telegrams and replied to them,' Jill pointed out.

'Maybe you were just lucky to have them replied to. Why don't you send another, just in case the last one didn't arrive.'

Jill brightened. 'Yes, I've got nothing to lose by doing that, have I?'

She was composing the telegram before taking it down to the telegraph office when there was a knock at the door of their dressing-room. Daley entered. It was obvious from his expression that he was a bearer of bad news.

'What is it?' demanded Letitia, who had quickly and accurately read his expression. 'Are McGee and Salmon dead?'

'No, but you two are,' replied Daley.

'What on earth are you talking about?' demanded Jill.

'Here.' Daley produced a copy of the *New York Argus*. The article on the front page was devoted to the train robbery which had taken place five days before. It stated that none of the Quail gang, who had been responsible for the robbery, had so far been apprehended. It concluded with a list of the victims of the disaster. Jill's and Letitia's names were prominent on the list. Daley had ringed them in pencil.

'How have they got our names?' demanded Jill. 'We're very much alive.'

'In fact I can vouch for two people,' said Letitia, patting her stomach.

'They must have got the names from the list of people who applied for tickets to travel on the train,' explained Daley. 'You gave your names to the ticket officer when you bought the tickets, I suppose?'

'Yes, we bought our tickets the day before,' confirmed Letitia.

'The ticket officer asked us our names. He entered them on the ticket,' stated Jill.

'And there was a duplicate counter-foil underneath,' concluded Letitia, triumphantly.

'The *Argus* must have been in contact with the ticket office and copied the entries on the ticket counterfoils,' stated Daley, thoughtfully.

Letitia smiled. 'Considering I'm dead I've never felt more alive in my life.'

'It's unlucky to joke about things like that,' said Jill, sharply.

'That isn't the end of the story,' said Daley, seriously.

'What do you mean?' demanded Letitia.

'It could be the reason why your boyfriends haven't come here to see you. They might have seen a list of people killed in the train robbery. They might have assumed that you two are dead.'

'What is the date on the newspaper?' demanded Jill.

'It's nearly a week old — 23 September,' replied Daley. 'One of the painters left it lying around. I only picked it up because the headline caught my eye.'

'Oh, my God!' said a distraught Letitia. 'We were thinking that McGee and Salmon would be arriving here any day. In fact they haven't come because they thought we were killed on the train.'

'It certainly looks that way,' concurred Daley.

'What are we going to do?' demanded Jill.

'There's only one thing to do,' stated a determined Letitia. 'We've got to go to that town where they're staying. What's its name?'

'Stoneville,' supplied Jill.

28

In the Taunton ranch the doctor was examining a corpse. The body was stretched out on a couch in the drawing-room. The doctor was a middle-aged man with a round face and a cheerful bedside manner.

'He certainly came to a sticky end,' he observed, wiping some of the blood from the corpse on to a towel which the housekeeper had supplied.

'I didn't shoot to kill him,' affirmed Salmon.

'I can see that,' said the doctor. 'You only shot his ear off.'

'Maybe the shock was too much for him. That was why he fell off his horse and died,' said McGee.

'He had a bad heart,' said the doctor. 'He could have died any time. He should have been taking things easy. Instead he kept this range war going with Stiles. I suppose you boys know all about that?'

'Yes, I think we found out the truth about it in the end,' said McGee.

'By the way, how are you?' asked the doctor. 'I believe you fell off your horse, too?'

'I'm all right, thanks,' McGee replied. 'I'm used to falling off horses.'

'The question is, what happens now?' demanded Salmon.

'You'll come into town to see the sheriff tomorrow morning. I'll make a sworn statement that your shot was not directly responsible for Taunton's death. You'll make a sworn statement describing exactly what did happen. And that should be that. I believe Taunton fired first at your friend?'

'That's right,' confirmed McGee.

The fourth person who was in the room, Jones, said, 'What happens to the ranch now?'

'It's up to the lawyer to find out who owns it. If Taunton left a Will then the new owner will have to be notified.'

'Taunton did have a nephew,' said Jones, thoughtfully. 'He used to come here from time to time to stay with him. He was a pleasant young man.'

'Maybe he'll be the new owner,' said the doctor. 'Anyhow you can check it out with the lawyer in town tomorrow.'

The following morning McGee, Salmon and Jones rode into Stoneville. When they reached Main Street Jones headed for the lawyer's office while McGee and Salmon went to the sheriff's office. They found that the doctor was already there.

'I've explained to the deputy what happened yesterday and how Taunton died,' stated the doctor.

'You'll have to make a signed statement,' the deputy informed Salmon. 'You can write, I suppose?'

'Of course he can,' supplied McGee. 'And he can read three-letter words as well.'

Salmon scowled at him. 'Give me a pen and paper,' he demanded.

While Salmon was writing out his statement McGee started examining the drawings of the Quail gang on the wall.

'They're not a very pretty lot are they?' he observed.

'There's a nice fat reward for their capture, dead or alive,' said the deputy.

Jones entered the office. 'It seems that Taunton's nephew could have inherited the ranch,' he announced.

'Let's hope he isn't as mad as his uncle,' stated the deputy.

'If you knew Taunton was mad, why didn't you do something about it?' demanded McGee.

'It was nothing to do with me,' replied the deputy. 'I wasn't in charge.'

'Well it's all over now anyhow,' McGee observed, as he continued examining the Quail gang.

'What are you two going to do?' asked Jones. 'Are you going to carry on working at the ranch?'

'I'm not sure,' answered McGee. 'We've been waiting for a telegram from our girlfriends. But so far we haven't received one.'

'The telegraph service isn't very reliable here. We're the end of the line and sometimes the messages don't come through.'

'The newspapers don't come through on time either,' stated the deputy. 'Sometimes we don't get them for a week or so after they're published.' He pointed to a couple of newspapers that were lying on a corner table.

'Have you almost finished?' queried McGee, as he picked up one of the newspapers.

'I've just got another few words,' Salmon informed him.

'This is the *New York Argus* which came out a week ago,' said McGee, casually, as he examined the newspaper.

'I told you that's how long it takes for them to get here,' stated the deputy sheriff.

Salmon finished his statement. 'There. That's that,' he stated. He glanced at McGee, expecting some flippant remark.

Instead his friend's face was as white as a sheet.

'You'd better read this,' he stated, handing him the copy of the *New York Argus*.

29

The Quail gang were riding west. They had been in the saddle for days and their tempers were getting frayed.

'How much further have we got to go?' demanded Ricardo.

'There's a town about ten miles ahead,' answered Quail.

'What's it called?' asked Ringer.

'Stoneville,' answered Quail.

'How far away is it from the Canadian border?' demanded Hislop.

'About thirty miles, I think,' answered Quail. 'There's one town between that and the Canadian border. It's called Cotterton.'

It was getting late in the evening. Shadows from the mountains were already beginning to spread over the valley.

'I hope there's a saloon in Stoneville,' said Lille. 'It's such a long time since

I've had a drink.'

'I hope there's a brothel in Stoneville,' said Ricardo. 'It's a long time since
I've had a woman.'

Everybody laughed.

About an hour later they approached
the town.

'It's not much of a place,' observed
Ringer.

'It's ideal for us,' said Quail, sharply.
'It's too far north for the news about
the train robbery to have reached here.'

'I wouldn't be too sure about that,'
said Lille, pointing upwards. 'The
telegraph has gone as far as this.'

'I expect they're all rubes here,' said
Hislop. 'Perhaps they haven't learned to
read.'

About half the gang were in favour of
camping up on the hillside. 'I think it
will be safer,' said Cleeves.

Stan Bryce agreed with him. 'We can
push on to Cotterton tomorrow. Then
reach the Canadian border the following day.'

'It's obvious some of you are in

167

favour of camping out tonight,' said Quail. 'In that case, since we're a democratic gang, we'd better have a vote on it.'

They voted and there were five in favour of camping out and, afterwards, pushing on to Cotterton.

The democratic decision was shattered by Ricardo's announcement.

'I'm not spending another night camping out. I'm fed up with waking up in the morning wet through. I've got a chance of a nice warm bed. And a beautiful woman to share it with me. I'm going to find a saloon and spend the night there.'

'I'll come with you,' said Lille. 'I don't think I can spend a night up in those mountains when I know there's some delicious beer in the saloons.'

'We've always stuck together so far,' stated Quail. 'It'll only mean camping out for another couple of nights.'

'I've had enough of sleeping out in the open, too,' said Hislop. 'The thought of a nice warm bath is too tempting. If you two are going into Stoneville, I'll join you.'

There were rumblings of discontent among the others. 'We've taken a democratic vote. I think we should stick to it,' said Cleeves.

'I don't think that one night is going to make any difference,' said Murphy. 'I'm all for enjoying myself tonight. It's wine, women and song for me, too. I'll join you three,' he stated positively.

'We'll be starting off early for Cotterton in the morning,' warned Quail.

'We'll join you there,' said Lille.

The four headed into town while the others took a mountain trail which would take them above Stoneville.

'They must be mad sleeping out for another night when they could be sitting in a comfortable saloon with a few drinks and a lovely *señorita*,' said Ricardo.

'Especially since we've got all this lovely money to spend,' said Hislop, tapping his saddle-bag.

'I've been looking forward to having some beer for the last two weeks,' stated Lille. 'The first few pints will go down as sweet as a nut.'

'Which saloon shall we go into?' demanded Murphy.

'That's easy. The first one we come to,' stated Ricardo.

The others laughed.

The saloon was named The Red Garter. However there was no sign of any women, let alone any wearing red garters. In fact the saloon was almost deserted. There was only the inevitable card players at a corner table. Apart from that there were two men sitting at a side table.

'There's nothing here,' said Ricardo. 'Let's move on to another saloon.'

'Hold on. Let's have a beer here first,' said Lille. 'I'm dying for a drink of beer.'

'All right,' agreed Ricardo. 'One drink, then we move on.'

The barman overheard their remarks. 'Things will liven up in an hour or so,' he promised them.

'What about women?' demanded Ricardo.

'Yes, there'll be a few of those, too,' stated the barman.

The two at the side table were too engrossed in their private conversation to notice the newcomers.

'They were coming to see us and they died for their loyalty,' said Salmon. His normal easygoing expression had changed. He now had a hard face which seemed to have aged him several years.

McGee's face too was drawn and haggard.

'Why did they have to come on the train?' he demanded.

'Because they loved us, that's why,' snarled Salmon. 'They loved us, and look what we did to them.'

'That's a bit strong,' retorted McGee. 'We weren't responsible for that gang blowing up the train.'

'No, but we were responsible for them coming West in the first place. If we'd stayed in New York, they'd never have come on the train. Then they would never have been killed.'

Ricardo and his companions glanced across at the two arguing.

'Hey, señores,' Ricardo called out to them. 'Will you join us in a drink? It looks as though you two could do with cheering up.'

McGee and Salmon glanced up at the four standing by the bar. For the first time they took in their faces. Gradually recognition dawned on them.

'It's four of the gang,' whispered Salmon.

'I think you're right,' confirmed McGee.

'The one who's just asked us for a drink is called Ricardo. He's Mexican. I can't remember the names of the others.'

'I think the name of the one with the thin face is Murphy,' said McGee.

Ricardo had been waiting impatiently for their answer to his offer of a drink. The four watched while the duo whispered. They weren't able to distinguish what they were saying. Not until the final sentence when McGee put too much emphasis on the last word of his sentence.

'They know who we are,' said Lille.

It was the signal for the four to dive for their guns. At the same time McGee and Salmon went for theirs.

The sound of gunfire echoed around the saloon. The bartender had dived behind the bar, taking the bottle of whiskey which had been on the bar in front of him. The four card players, whose movements until then had been slow and deliberate dived down below their table with startling rapidity. When the first flurry of movement had stopped there were three men lying on the floor by the bar. It was obvious from their prone positions that they were no longer going to take any further interest in the proceedings. The fourth member of the gang was also lying on the floor, but the combination of the blood from his wound and his groans told its own tale. They indicated that he might have a reasonable chance of living.

McGee and Salmon approached him. At the same time the card-players under the table rose warily.

'What's your name?' demanded Salmon, as they surveyed the wounded outlaw.

'Hislop,' he replied, through gritted teeth. 'Get me a doctor. Please.'

'All in good time,' said McGee. 'First we want you to tell us about the rest of the gang.'

'If you don't get a doctor to take out this bullet, I'll bleed to death,' said Hislop.

'I'll fetch a doctor,' said one of the card-school.

'Stay where you are,' said McGee, threateningly. The man froze instantly. 'First of all you're going to tell us what we want to know,' McGee addressed the remark to Hislop.

'They're camped somewhere up on the side of the mountain. I don't know exactly where. Tomorrow at dawn they're going to make their way to

Cotterton. Then they plan to go on to the Canadian border.'

'How many are there?' demanded Salmon.

'Five. Fetch a doctor, please,' pleaded Hislop.

McGee nodded to the card-player, who shot out through the door. The bartender, who had once again assumed his usual position behind the bar, said;

'Would you gentlemen like a drink? I would take it as a privilege if you will accept it. I have never see such shooting in the twenty years I've been a barman.'

'We'll just have one,' said McGee. 'Then we have some more work to do.'

30

The following morning they were on the trail early to Cotterton. They had knocked the deputy sheriff up in his house after the shooting in The Red Garter. They had explained that they had killed three of the Quail gang and that there was one who was wounded and the doctor was attending to him.

'His name's Hislop,' volunteered Salmon.

The deputy's comment after absorbing the information was: 'I never thought you boys were killers.'

'Neither did we. Until an hour ago,' supplied McGee.

'The bastards killed our girlfriends,' explained Salmon. 'They were on the train that they blew up to rob it,' said McGee.

The deputy's parting shot was: 'If you two come back alive from Cotterton, there'll be a nice fat reward in bounty money for killing the three so far.'

The two rode along the trail in silence. The events of the previous night had changed their lives irrevocably. Their girlfriends were now dead. They knew it would take a long time for them to become reconciled to that fact. On the other hand they had killed three of the gang who had killed them, and put a fourth out of action. In a small way they felt they had avenged the blowing-up of the train.

'There are still five to catch,' said Salmon.

McGee felt that his friend had been reading his mind.

'At least we know who they are. We've got the element of surprise,' stated McGee.

'We're not going to do it on our own, are we?' demanded Salmon.

'No, the odds would be too big. Two against five,' replied McGee, thought-fully. 'We'll try and get the sheriff on our side. The deputy said that he was a good man.'

They reached Cotterton in late afternoon after pushing their horses at a fast pace all day.

'It's a good thing we are used to riding,' stated McGee. 'I'd never have done that a month ago.'

Cotterton turned out to be a lot smaller than Stoneville. They passed a saloon named The Setting Sun and soon arrived at the sheriff's office. They dismounted, tied up their horses and knocked at the door.

'Come in,' said a voice.

The sheriff was seated behind an old mahogany desk. He was a big man who was still on the right side of middle age.

'What can I do for you fellers?' he demanded.

'We've got some information about the Quail gang,' said McGee.

'And who are they when they're alive?' demanded the sheriff.

'Not as many as they used to be,' said McGee. 'Some of them are dead.'

'You interest me,' said the sheriff. 'By the way my name's Hal Smith.'

McGee and Salmon introduced themselves. They told their story. Hal listened without interruption. In the end, he said:

'Two against four. You did very well.'

'We used to be sharpshooters in a circus,' explained McGee.

There was a knock at the door and a woman entered. She was a stunning redhead. Hal introduced her as his wife, Cathy.

'I'm afraid I might be late coming home tonight,' Hal told her. 'We have some unfinished business to see to.'

She glanced suspiciously at McGee and Salmon.

'I suppose these gentlemen are the cause of it,' she said, icily.

'I might as well explain,' said Hal, resignedly. He told her as much of the story as he could while McGee and Salmon completed the picture.

'I'm sorry about your girlfriends,' she said at the end of the explanation. 'I hope you get the bastards.'

'So do we, darling,' said Hal.

When she had left Hal announced that he was going to check his guns. 'At least we'll have the benefit of surprise on our side,' he announced, as he went into the back room.

He would have been shocked to discover that in fact that was not the case. When the five remaining members of the gang had risen early and, having devoured their usual breakfast of beans and coffee, were about to set off, they discovered that there was a snag. Cleeves's horse was lame and there was no way he would be able to ride him to Cotterton.

'You'll have to go into Stoneville to get a fresh horse from the livery stable,' said Quail. 'We'll wait here for you. By the way, you might as well pick up Lille and the others while you're there. We can all ride together to Cotterton.'

Nearly two hours later Cleeves returned. The gang were becoming very restless by that time. Several of them had voiced the opinion that they should all go into Stoneville to find out what had happened to Cleeves. However he did appear over the brow of the hill eventually. The members of the gang watched expectantly. But there was no sign of anyone accompanying him.

'What happened to Lille and the others?' demanded Quail.

Cleeves explained that he had gone to the livery stable to buy a horse. The man in charge of the stable, a garrulous old man, started to tell him about the shoot-out in The Red Garter saloon the previous night. When the old man had mentioned that the shoot-out involved members of the Quail gang he had Cleeves's complete attention.

'What happened?' demanded Quail.

'Lille, Ricardo and Murphy are dead. Hislop is being held by the deputy sheriff. He's been wounded, but it seems as though he will live.'

'Three dead,' said Stan Bryce, disbelievingly.

'There's no doubt about it. I called in

at The Red Garter saloon and the barman confirmed it. He said the two who shot them were the quickest gunslingers he had seen in all the years he had been working behind a bar.'

There was silence while the others digested the facts. Finally Frank Bryce asked, 'What are we going to do?'

'We're going to put two and two together,' answered Quail.

'What do you mean?' demanded Ringer.

'You say Hislop is injured?' demanded Quail.

'Yes, but not seriously.'

'Just enough to have told the law about our plans,' pursued Quail, remorselessly.

'Yes, I suppose so,' answered Cleeves, as it began to dawn on him what his chief was driving at.

'Hislop was always a coward,' stated Quail. 'He'd give our plans away without blinking an eye. He would have told the law that we intended going on to Cotterton.'

'So what are we going to do?' demanded Frank Bryce.

'We're going into Cotterton to avenge the three of our gang who have been killed. The two gunslingers will have ridden ahead thinking they can surprise us. But we'll have the element of surprise on our side. Did the saloon-keeper say what the two men looked like?'

'He said that one of the men was a very big man, while the other was smaller. He had found out that their names were McGee and Salmon.'

31

McGee and Salmon had been waiting in the sheriff's office for a couple of hours. There was no sign of any riders approaching the town. Darkness had began to edge in. In half an hour it would be completely dark and it would be doubtful whether the remaining members of the gang would be coming into town. They might decide to camp up on the mountainside and come into town tomorrow.

Hal's wife, Cathy, interrupted their vigil by bringing them some food. It was only bread and cheese, but the bread was home-made and tasted delicious. She kept watch on the main street while they ate their food.

When they had finished, Hal said, 'Cathy is a good shot with a gun. But not in the same league as you two boys. However she's great with a throwing knife. She can kill a jack rabbit at sixty paces.'

'I had to be able to do so,' she explained. 'I was brought up living up in the mountains. I had to learn to kill a jack rabbit or we'd go hungry.'

After Cathy had left they resumed their vigil. Hal sitting by the open door.

'If they come in now they'll probably stop at the first saloon they come to,' stated Hal. 'It's called The Setting Sun.'

McGee asked a question which had been worrying him since they had arrived. 'Haven't you got a deputy?' he demanded.

'I used to have one, but he decided it was so quiet here, that he upped and left,' explained Hal. 'This is a small law-abiding town. We don't get much trouble here. But it looks as though we might have some tonight,' he concluded, grimly.

The duo correctly inferred from his change of tone that the Quail gang had come into sight. They joined him at the doorway. There was just enough light for them to see five riders in the distance.

'We'll wait and see where they stop,' said Hal. 'You two go back inside.'

They waited anxiously while Hal kept up a commentary of the riders' progress. 'They're passing the livery stable, they're passing the coffee-shop, they're passing the Wells Fargo office, they're coming to The Setting Sun.' He couldn't keep the excitement out of his voice. 'They're stopping there.' There was a pause. The two inside held their breath. Finally Hal said. 'They're dismounting. They're tying up their horses, and they're going inside.'

'We've got them,' exclaimed McGee.

Hal came back inside the office. 'Now this is what we do,' he informed them. 'You point them out to me. Although probably I'll have no difficulty in recognizing them, since I know all the regulars in The Setting Sun. I challenge them and tell them I'm arresting them. They'll probably go for their guns. That's where you two will come in. We'll have the element of surprise on our side.'

It was now completely dark as the three made their way up Main Street towards the saloon. There was enough light from the moon to show them the way. In addition there were the lamps which burned cheerfully in the front window of most of the houses. McGee's and Salmon's revolvers were in their holsters. The sheriff, however, was carrying a Winchester rifle.

'I've done this many times before,' said Hal, 'but I always get a funny feeling in the pit of my stomach when I do it again.'

They came to the front door of the saloon. Hal glanced at the two to make sure that they were ready. They assured him that they were. Hal pushed open the door of the saloon and stepped inside. McGee and Salmon joined him. Their eyes eagerly devoured the couple of dozen or so men who were in the bar. They registered their disbelief when they saw that none of the Quail gang was there.

'They're not here,' said an amazed Salmon.

'It's a trap,' cried Hal. 'Get down.' As they dived to the floor they were met with a hail of bullets from a balcony above.

For a big man Hal moved with surprising speed. It was this lightning reaction that saved him from being picked off by one of the gang above. It did not completely come to his aid however, since he felt a familiar tug at his arm which told him that one of the gang's bullets had hit his right arm.

McGee and Salmon too hit the floor with lightning speed. Since they were trained performers their years of practice probably saved their lives. They escaped being the victims of the volley from above.

They quickly realized, however, that they were still in imminent danger. The five on the balcony were adjusting their positions so that they could get final telling shots at them. When the two had hit the floor they had automatically drawn their guns at the same time. McGee summed up the situation quickly. He started shooting. Not at the five who were concealed on the balcony above, but at the lamps which were dotted around the saloon. Salmon saw his plan and began to follow suit. When the next round of bullets came from the outlaw's revolvers, they were very wide of their targets.

'Well done, boys,' said Hal, appreciatively.

'What do we do next?' asked McGee.

'We smoke them out,' said Hal.

'How do you intend to do that?' asked Salmon.

The drinkers in the bar, having realized that they were in the middle of a gunfight, were rushing for the door. Some, even in the moment of danger, found time to swallow their drink before leaving.

'Come on,' said Hal. 'Join the crowd.'

The two obeyed and accompanied by

Hal they soon found themselves outside.

'There's only this one entrance to the
saloon,' said Hal. 'The gang are bound
to come out this way.'

'But we might have to stay here for
days,' complained Salmon.

'I don't think so,' said Hal. He began
to give instructions to those who had
gathered outside. 'I want you men to
gather some bundles of straw. Put it
around the building. When I tell you,
set fire to it. There's a gang of killers
inside known as the Quail gang. There's
a big reward out for their capture. If
you men help to catch them, I'll see
that you'll have a share of the reward.'

The men went to work willingly.

'Are you sure you're doing the right
thing by burning the place down?'
demanded Salmon.

'I've always wanted to get rid of this
place,' said Hal. 'The owners have been
using it as a base to smuggle goods,
whiskey and guns over the border.
Here's my chance.'

'You're hurt,' said McGee, noticing the blood on Hal's arm.

'It's only a scratch,' said Hal.

The men worked on enthusiastically collecting their straw. Much of it came from the livery stable. In less than half an hour they had collected enough to satisfy Hal.

'I'm going to light it now,' he informed the duo. 'You two take up your positions by the door. When the five come out, shoot them. Don't give them a chance to shoot at you. I won't be able to do any shooting because of my damaged right arm. So I'm depending on you two.'

Hal went round the saloon lighting the bales. Soon they were blazing merrily. The flames licked up the wooden sides of the saloon. The fire had attracted the other inhabitants of the town who came out, some in their night-attire, to see what was happening.

'There are some dangerous men inside,' yelled Hal. 'Keep back.'

It didn't take the dangerous men

long to realize that if they stayed in the saloon they would be burned alive. They came out through the front at a rush. Quick as they were, McGee and Salmon were quicker. They shot two each as they came out.

However it left Quail alive. Before either of the two could change their aim he prepared to dispatch McGee to his Maker. Everything happened in a split second. There was the whistle of a knife and to McGee's surprise Quail, instead of firing at him, was clutching at the knife which was sticking out of his heart.

'It's nice to see that I haven't lost my touch,' said Cathy, who had material-ized by McGee's side.

'I'll never be able to thank you enough,' said McGee.

'It's we who should be thanking you,' said Cathy. 'Look at him,' she said, pointing to Hal, who presented a happy, if rather smoke-blackened figure. 'He's never enjoyed himself so much for ages.'

After the excitement of the last two days, the duo's ride to Stoneville was an anticlimax. They had spent an entertaining night as guests of Hal and Cathy. They had talked late into the night, with McGee and Salmon entertaining their hosts with stories about their exploits in the circus and the characters they had met.

With heavy hearts they had to take their leave. Cathy had hugged them both.

'If you're ever in this part of the world again, look us up,' she had commanded.

★ ★ ★

At last they were approaching Stoneville.

'We'd better see the deputy sheriff,' said McGee. 'We'd better tell him that it's all over.'

They entered the sheriff's office. The deputy didn't seem surprised to see them.

'We've come to report about what happened in Cotterton,' said McGee.

'Listen, I'm just closing the office for the day,' said the deputy. 'Why don't you two come home with me. My wife's a good cook. I expect you could do with something to eat. You can tell me all about it then.'

The two willingly agreed. They had been in the saddle all day and they were hungry.

When they reached the deputy's house, he told them to go ahead inside while he tied up their horses. They went inside, where they received the biggest shock they had ever had in their lives. Letitia and Jill were sitting in the drawing-room.

The expressions on McGee's and Salmon's faces sent the girls into peals of laughter.

'But — but — we thought you were dead,' stammered Salmon.

'Come and sit down by me,' said Jill. 'I'll show you that I'm still alive.'

'What about you?' Letitia addressed

the remark to the still bemused McGee. 'What have you been up to?'

He came out of his trance. 'I won a rodeo. Stopped a range war. And killed most of the Quail gang,' he replied.

She obviously didn't believe him. She smiled and patted the empty seat by her side. 'Now come and tell me exactly what you *have* been up to,' she said.

THE END

We do hope that you have enjoyed reading this large print book.

Did you know that all of our titles are available for purchase?

We publish a wide range of high quality large print books including:
Romances, Mysteries, Classics
General Fiction
Non Fiction and Westerns

Special interest titles available in large print are:
The Little Oxford Dictionary
Music Book, Song Book
Hymn Book, Service Book

Also available from us courtesy of Oxford University Press:
Young Readers' Dictionary
(large print edition)
Young Readers' Thesaurus
(large print edition)

For further information or a free brochure, please contact us at:
Ulverscroft Large Print Books Ltd.,
The Green, Bradgate Road, Anstey,
Leicester, LE7 7FU, England.
Tel: (00 44) **0116 236 4325**
Fax: (00 44) **0116 234 0205**

Other titles in the
Linford Western Library:

DEAD IS FOR EVER

Amy Sadler

After rescuing Hope Bennett from the clutches of two trailbums, Sam Carver made a serious mistake. He killed one of the outlaws, and reckoned on collecting the bounty on Lew Daggett. But catching Sam off-guard, Daggett made off with the girl, leaving Sam for dead. However, he was only grazed and once he came to, he set out in search of Hope. When he eventually found her, he was forced into a dramatic showdown with his life on the line.

SMOKING STAR

B. J. Holmes

In the one-horse town of Medicine Bluff two men were dead. Sheriff Jack Starr didn't need the badge on his chest to spur him into tracking the killer. He had his own reason for seeking justice, a reason no-one knew. It drove him to take a journey into the past where he was to discover something else that was to add even greater urgency to the situation — to stop Montana's rivers running red with blood.

THE WIND WAGON

Troy Howard

Sheriff Al Corning was as tough as they came and with his four seasoned deputies he kept the peace in Laramie — at least until the squatters came. To fend off starvation, the settlers took some cattle off the cowmen, including Jonas Lefler. A hard, unforgiving man, Lefler retaliated with lynchings. Things got worse when one of the squatters revealed he was a former Texas lawman — and no mean shooter. Could Sheriff Corning prevent further bloodshed?

CABEL

Paul K. McAfee

Josh Cabel returned home from the
Civil War to find his family all
murdered by rioting members of
Quantrill's band. The hunt for the
killers led Josh to Colorado City
where, after months of searching, he
finally settled down to work on a
ranch nearby. He saved the life of an
Indian, who led him to a cache of
weapons waiting for Sitting Bull's
attack on the Whites. His involve-
ment threw Cabel into grave danger.
When the final confrontation came,
who had the fastest — and deadlier
— draw?

RIVERBOAT

Alan C. Porter

When Rufus Blake died he was
found to be carrying a gold bar
from a Confederate gold shipment
that had disappeared twenty years
before. This inspires Wes Hardiman
and Ben Travis to swap horse and
trail for a riverboat, the *River
Queen*, on the Mississippi, in an
effort to find the missing gold. Cord
Duval is set on destroying the *River
Queen* and he has the power and
the gunmen to do it. Guns blaze as
Hardiman and Travis attempt to
unravel the mystery and stay alive.

McKINNEY'S LAW

Mike Stotter

McKinney didn't count on coming across a dead body in the middle of Texas. He was about to become involved in an ever-deepening mystery. The renegade Comanche warrior, Black Eagle, was on the loose, creating havoc; he didn't appear in McKinney's plans at all, not until the Comanche forced himself into his life. The US Army gave McKinney some relief to his problems, but it also added to them, and with two old friends McKinney set about bringing justice through his own law.